A RC
PUNISHMENT

Barbara Cartland

Barbara Cartland Ebooks Ltd

ISBNs

9781782139836 EPUB

978-1-78867-710-3 PAPERBACK

Book design by M-Y Books
m-ybooks.co.uk

THE BARBARA CARTLAND ETERNAL COLLECTION

The Barbara Cartland Eternal Collection is the unique opportunity to collect all five hundred of the timeless beautiful romantic novels written by the world's most celebrated and enduring romantic author.

Named the Eternal Collection because Barbara's inspiring stories of pure love, just the same as love itself, the books will be published on the internet at the rate of four titles per month until all five hundred are available.

The Eternal Collection, classic pure romance available worldwide for all time .

THE LATE DAME BARBARA CARTLAND

Barbara Cartland, who sadly died in May 2000 at the grand age of ninety eight, remains one of the world's most famous romantic novelists. With worldwide sales of over one billion, her outstanding 723 books have been translated into thirty six different languages, to be enjoyed by readers of romance globally.

Writing her first book 'Jigsaw' at the age of 21, Barbara became an immediate bestseller. Building upon this initial success, she wrote continuously throughout her life, producing bestsellers for an astonishing 76 years. In addition to Barbara Cartland's legion of fans in the UK and across Europe, her books have always been immensely popular in the USA. In 1976 she achieved the unprecedented feat of having books at numbers 1 & 2 in the prestigious B. Dalton Bookseller bestsellers list.

Although she is often referred to as the 'Queen of Romance', Barbara Cartland also wrote several historical biographies, six autobiographies and numerous theatrical plays as well as books on life, love, health and cookery. Becoming one of Britain's most popular media personalities and dressed in her trademark pink, Barbara spoke on radio and television about social and political issues, as well as making many public appearances.

In 1991 she became a Dame of the Order of the British Empire for her contribution to literature and her work for humanitarian and charitable causes.

Known for her glamour, style, and vitality Barbara Cartland became a legend in her own lifetime. Best remembered for her wonderful romantic novels and loved by millions of readers worldwide, her books remain treasured for their heroic heroes, plucky heroines and traditional values. But above all, it was Barbara Cartland's overriding belief in the positive power of love to help, heal and improve the quality of life for everyone that made her truly unique.

AUTHOR'S NOTE

Flogging was, in the Royal Navy, with the terrible "cat o' nine tails", the standard punishment for centuries.

Startling facts from the ship's logs show that it was no deterrent. It is also obvious that the men of the eighteenth century were inordinately tough.

On Nelson's flagship *The Victory,* on watch in Toulon and later in the War, between January and July 105 men were flogged, 13 of them more than once.

One of them was punished four times in this brief space of time: January 10th with 12 lashes, March 5th with 36, April 5th – 48, and May 24th – 48.

His offences were theft, drunkenness, more drunkenness and more theft. Other common crimes were insolence, uncleanliness, sleeping on watch, fighting, neglect and disobedience. Nelson's Flag Captain Hardy was a stern man, and the Admiral did not interfere with the running of the ship. But Collingwood, who was ten years older than Nelson, treated his Captains as 'assistants'.

As Nelson grew old, he rarely sanctioned flogging, and discipline did not suffer as one of the crew wrote,

"A look of displeasure from him was as bad as a dozen at the gangway from another man."

In 1871, flogging was 'suspended in peacetime' and eight years later it was suspended in wartime, and it was ten more before the Army gave it up.

CHAPTER ONE
1860

"Darling Stanwin, if only I could marry you, how happy we would be."

The Marquis, who, feeling somewhat fatigued, was lying comfortably against the lace pillows, did not reply.

He had heard women say this so often that his mind had even ceased to react. He knew that if he told the truth, the last person he would wish to marry was the soft clinging creature whose head now rested against his shoulder.

"No lover has ever been as wonderful as you, darling, however much the poets may extol them!"

This again was something the Marquis had heard before, and he merely responded by pulling Lady Hester Dendall a little closer to him.

As he did so, it was a satisfaction to remember that her husband was on a special mission to Paris, so there was no chance of his being involved in similar circumstances to that which he had had to face a fortnight ago.

Then the Earl of Castleton, returning unexpectedly to his house in Park Lane and finding the Marquis and his wife in a compromising situation, had called him out.

Despite the fact that duels were frowned upon both by the Queen and the Prince Consort, they met in Green Park and, most unjustly, it was the Earl of Castleton who had been wounded in the arm, while the Marquis had got off scot-free.

That was what usually happened where the Marquis was concerned, and neither his seconds nor his friends were surprised.

But the Earl had walked off, swearing that sooner or later he would 'get even' with him.

The Marquis in consequence had been warned that he had a dangerous enemy, but he had just laughed somewhat cynically.

So many husbands had threatened him at one time or another, and because he was a crack shot, he had always managed to come out the victor in every duel and was afterwards completely unimpressed by anything they could say about him.

"I love you! *I love you!*" Lady Hester said passionately. "But if you are unfaithful to me again, as you were with Sheila Castleton, I think I shall kill you!"

The Marquis laughed.

"What with – a bow and arrow?"

"Do not be so unkind," Lady Hester protested. "You know, dearest Stanwin, that I adore you, and it is agony to think that you have even looked at another woman!"

It was extraordinary, the Marquis thought, settling himself more comfortably, that women were never content with what they had, and always wanted more.

For Hester to be begging him to be faithful to her was rather like asking Niagara Falls to dry up, or King Canute ordering the tide to turn back.

All through his life the Marquis had found a pretty face irresistible and, although he was extremely fastidious, he found it impossible not to aim to win where other men had failed.

Granted that in the Social set in which he moved, the women on whom he bestowed his favours were experienced, sophisticated and in every case determined to attract his attention.

It was rather unfortunate, he thought, that while what to him was merely an *affaire de coeur,* the women in the case inevitably became serious and fell in love with him.

"I love you! I love you!"

He had heard the words repeated and re-repeated by soft voices until it was to him as familiar as the winds blowing outside the window or the birds singing in the trees.

"Think how happy we would be," Lady Hester was saying rather dreamily. "We would undoubtedly be the most handsome couple in the whole of London and, wearing the Weybourne tiara, I would be the outstanding Peeress at the Opening of Parliament."

Her fantasy was tiresomely the same as had been indulged in by a number of other women, and the Marquis merely closed his eyes and thought that as he was sleepy it was time he returned home to his own bed.

"I must go, Hester," he said in a slow, lazy drawl, which, for some reason he had never been able to understand, women found irresistible.

"Go?"

Lady Hester's voice rose in a scream as she spoke.

"Oh, no! How can you leave me? How can I let you go? Kiss me! Oh, Stanwin, *kiss me!*"

The Marquis, however, resolutely got out of bed.

He thought as he did so that the room was rather airless and Hester as usual had used too much of her favourite French perfume.

It certainly smelt exotic. At the same time, he had a sudden longing for the chill of the night, or the breeze that usually comes up from the river with the dawn.

Without thinking, without being aware that his body had the athletic proportions of a Greek god, he walked to the chair on which he had thrown his evening clothes and started to put them on.

Lady Hester, with her dark hair falling over her shoulders, watched him from the bed.

She was very beautiful, in fact the most beautiful brunette in the whole of London, and as her Irish blood had given her brilliant blue eyes, she was outstanding in every ballroom in which she appeared.

The daughter of an impoverished Irish Earl, she had made what was thought of as a 'brilliant marriage' to the wealthy Sir Anthony Dendall who was an up-and-coming young politician.

In fact, in *White's Club* they were already betting he would be in the next Cabinet.

Sir Anthony had been head-over-heels in love with his beautiful wife when he had married her, but as he was politically ambitious, he had soon found there were more things to interest him outside his own house, than in.

This had resulted in Lady Hester taking a series of lovers, none of them, however, she admitted to herself, so important, so attractive, as the Marquis of Weybourne.

She had been determined that he would become her lover from the first moment she had set eyes on him.

It was a year before he had finally succumbed to her wiles and he had made her no promises of not finding other women equally interesting.

Wildly passionate besides being wildly in love, Lady Hester found it an intolerable torture to know that she never was sure what the Marquis was doing.

The news of his duel with the Earl of Castleton had been a bombshell, and while she knew she should have nothing more to do with the Marquis after such unfaithfulness, she found it impossible not to forgive him even though she would never forget.

There was a little edge to her voice as she asked now,

"Are you dining with me tomorrow night?"

"I cannot remember," the Marquis said casually as he inserted a pearl stud into his evening shirt.

"What do you mean?" Hester asked sharply.

"I have a feeling that I have promised to dine with Devonshire – or was it somebody else?"

"If it is a dinner party, perhaps I also have an invitation," Lady Hester said not very hopefully, "but, anyway, you will come to me afterwards?"

There was a little pause while the Marquis concentrated on tying his tie in the mirror that was over the carved marble mantelpiece.

"Shall I say I will think about it," he said with a smile as he realised Hester was waiting for his answer.

"How can you be so cruel, so unkind to me?"

She sprang out of bed as she spoke and, naked, with her hair falling over her shoulders, ran towards him to fling her arms round his neck.

She looked exquisitely lovely as she did so, but the Marquis merely held her away from him.

"The trouble with you," he said, "is that you are insatiable. You do not want one man, but a regiment of them!"

"If they all looked like you and made love like you," Lady Hester replied, "I should be only too happy!"

She flung back her head as she spoke and looking up at him invited his kisses.

He looked down at her with a faint glint of amusement in his eyes and a slightly cynical twist to his lips.

Then he picked her up in his arms and carrying her across the room dumped her down on the bed.

"Behave yourself, Hester!" he said. "If you are very good I will either call on you late tomorrow evening, or perhaps we might dine the day after."

She gave a little cry of joy and held out her arms to him.

"Kiss me once more before you go, darling Stanwin," she pleaded.

The Marquis however walked back to the chair to pick up his evening coat and shrug himself into it.

It fitted without a wrinkle over his square shoulders, making his small waist and narrow hips seem more elegant than ever.

Lady Hester drew in her breath.

She had only to look at the Marquis to feel her heart beating frantically and her breath coming quickly from between her lips.

"Kiss me, *please, kiss me,*" she repeated.

"I have been caught that way before," the Marquis replied.

He was well aware that if a man bent over a woman who was lying in bed she could easily pull him down on top of her, and then there would be no escape.

Instead, he took one of her outstretched hands in his, kissed it lightly and, without saying any more, went from the room, closing the door quietly behind him.

When he had gone, Lady Hester gave a little whimper of exasperation before she slipped under the bedclothes.

It was always the same, she thought, when the Marquis left her and she was never quite certain when she would see him again.

She had told herself a thousand times that he was as wildly in love with her as she was with him, and yet a fortnight ago there had been the episode of Sheila Castleton, and she rather suspected there had been other women before her.

"I love him! *I love him!*" she declared defiantly to the empty room, "and I swear I will never lose him!"

*

As he went down the stairs that were almost in darkness, the Marquis thought that Hester was becoming more and more importunate, and sooner or later Dendall was certain to hear of it.

There was going to be some interfering, meddling busybody ready to inform him of what was going on in his absence, and following the duel with the Earl of Castleton the Marquis felt that if he had any sense he should behave with more caution in the future.

He had known he was taking a chance in having supper with Sheila Castleton when she invited him to do so when the Earl was in England but, according to his wife, not returning from the country until the following day.

The Marquis had cursed himself for being so careless when everybody was aware that the Earl was extremely jealous and liable to return unexpectedly just to find out what his wife did in his absence.

It was extremely fortunate, the Marquis thought, that he had been on the point of leaving the Countess's bedroom when the Earl had walked in.

He was dressed, so he was not in quite such an ignominious position as he would have been a half hour earlier.

But the Countess was still in bed, naked, and at the first sight of her husband she was so surprised that she sat up in bed, giving a shrill scream, which did nothing to help the situation.

If the Earl had had a pistol in his hand, the Marquis knew that he would have undoubtedly fired it at him.

Instead, with what was admirable self-control considering the violence of his feelings, the Earl told him to get out of his house – and that he would avenge himself in the usual manner at dawn in the customary place in Green Park, where they were unlikely to be seen.

"I intend to kill you, Weybourne," he said, "so if you wish to say your prayers, you should start them now!"

The Marquis thought it best in the circumstances not to argue or enrage the Earl any further.

He merely left the bedroom with as much dignity as he could muster and walked deliberately slowly down the stairs into the hall.

He was aware as he did so that the Earl was watching him from the landing and that the night footman, who was opening the front door for him, looked white and shaken.

By the time he had changed his clothes and woken two of his friends to act as seconds, he only just had time to reach Green Park at the appointed hour.

"Why, in the name of the devil, do you want to fight Castleton?" Harry Melville had asked.

He had known the Marquis all his life.

They had been at Eton together, served in the same regiment, and he was in fact the only person in whom the Marquis ever confided.

"You know the answer to that," he replied lazily.

"I knew that Sheila Castleton was after you," Harry Melville said, "which is not surprising, but you must be aware that the Earl is both jealous and vindictive and it is a mistake to have him as an enemy."

The Marquis shrugged his shoulders.

"He is only one of many," he said, "and he should look after his wife more competently if he wants to keep her to himself!"

Harry Melville laughed.

"Really, Stanwin, you know as well as I do that unless husbands lock chastity belts on their wives every time they leave them, there is no other way of keeping them out of your arms!"

The Marquis did not reply.

He never boasted of his conquests and disliked talking about them, even to Harry.

At the same time, because he was so often in difficulties with jealous husbands, Harry was invaluable to him in many ways.

"This is the fourth duel you have fought in the last two years," Harry was saying, "and quite frankly, Stanwin, I am fed up with having to get out of a warm bed to watch you appease some wretched husband's honour. The result always is that he will have his arm in a sling for three or four weeks while you walk about unscathed!"

"Castleton is supposed to be a good shot!" the Marquis remarked.

"But not as good as you!" Harry replied.

Which of course, proved to be the truth.

Sometimes the Marquis wondered if it was worthwhile, but at the same time he knew that even if he ceased to pursue pretty women, they would still continue to pursue him.

Hester had lasted much longer than most of them, but this was due to her persistence rather than the Marquis's.

She amused him, she was witty and spiteful in an entertaining manner, besides being like a tigress when they made love.

Sheila Castleton had been different and, if the Marquis were truthful, somewhat disappointing.

She was beautiful, there was no doubt about that, but she did not stimulate the same fires that Hester could do so effectively.

The Marquis knew that as far as he was concerned, the Earl of Castleton need have no fear that he would continue to covet his wife.

As Sir Anthony Dendall's house in Park Street was only a very short distance from his own house in Grosvenor Square, the Marquis had sent away his carriage and walked home.

He enjoyed the exercise, the fresh air and the feeling that he was free for the moment, from clinging arms and hungry lips.

It was something he often felt after hours of lovemaking, and usually his thoughts then were of the country, his horses and his intention of winning every classic race with them.

Tonight, as he walked along, he told himself that he would be happy not to see so much of Hester in the future. In fact, he decided he had no intention of seeing her late tomorrow evening, or dining with her the following night.

'She is not going to like it,' he thought.

He found himself thinking of the undoubted attractions of a very pretty ballerina he had noticed the other night when he had attended a new ballet at Covent Garden.

He played with the idea that he might ask her to have supper with him tomorrow after the performance.

He was quite confident she would accept, whatever other arrangements she had made, but it struck him that at closer quarters she might be disappointing.

It was sad to think that many women were, whether one saw them on the stage or in the ballroom.

So often their allure seemed to come off with their gowns, and he continually found himself thinking it had all been a waste of time.

'What am I looking for?' he asked. 'What do I expect?'

He told himself he was being unusually introspective, and it must be because he was tired.

His lips twisted in the cynical way that his friends knew so well as he thought that no one could spend several hours with Hester without being tired.

He reached his house in Grosvenor Square and the sound of his footsteps alerted the night footman quickly to open the front door.

He had been having great difficulty in keeping himself awake until his Master returned.

He thought now, as the Marquis walked in, giving him his tall hat and cane as he did so, that with any luck he would have a couple of hours sleep before the housemaids came bustling into the hall to clean and polish.

"Goodnight, Henry!" the Marquis said as he started to climb the stairs.

"'Night, My Lord!" Henry replied respectfully.

He put the Marquis's hat and cane down on a chest and, having locked the front door, he settled himself comfortably in the padded chair, which was specially designed to keep out the cold of the long winter nights, and closed his eyes.

*

The Marquis, in his own bed, found himself unexpectedly wide awake.

He was thinking that he was bored with London and if he went away to Weybourne Park for a few days he would enjoy himself more than attending the endless assemblies, balls and receptions that were always part of the London Season.

He knew if he went away without any warning, a dozen hostesses would be extremely angry at his non-appearance at their balls, and those who expected him to dinner would be even more annoyed.

As for Hester… he shrugged philosophically.

Hester would miss him, and he was sorry if he upset her. At the same time, he knew with an insight that never failed him that their *affaire de coeur* was at an end.

The Marquis was usually ruthless and abrupt at the cessation of his love affairs simply because he found it impossible to pretend what he did not feel.

He expected perfection in everything around him, and therefore where his love affairs were concerned, he had long given up expecting anything sensational.

At the same time, when the fire of desire had to be slightly forced, he knew that the end was in sight.

He found that Hester was not only becoming too demanding and too monotonous in what she said, but also too clinging.

Being a strong character, the Marquis liked to dominate, and he did not like the woman to 'make the running'. He wanted to be the hunter, not the hunted.

Because Hester was so overwhelmingly in love with him, she had ceased to let him take the initiative, and that, he knew, was something, if he were truthful, he found intolerable.

'I will go to the country,' he decided, and knew as he did so that it would soften the blow when Hester found out he no longer desired her.

Although she would undoubtedly bombard him with letters, to which he had no intention of replying, she would gradually he hoped, become aware that their association was at an end.

'I will drive down with my new team,' the Marquis decided, and fell asleep.

*

The morning however threw the Marquis's plans into confusion.

He was called by his valet at the usual hour of eight o'clock.

He was just about to give the order for his chaise to be brought round in an hour's time when his valet said,

"There's a note for Your Lordship that's just arrived from the Palace."

"From the Palace?" the Marquis queried.

Havers produced a silver salver on which reposed a white envelope bearing the Royal Insignia.

The Marquis wondered what this could portend.

He opened it somewhat tentatively to find that it was signed by the Queen's Private Secretary informing him that Her Majesty would grant him an audience at noon today.

As the Marquis had not asked for an audience with the Queen, he was aware this was a Royal Command.

He felt uncomfortably that it was something he should have expected of her.

Because he was quick-witted and extremely intelligent, the Marquis guessed without being told that the Earl of Castleton had taken his revenge in a more subtle manner than by killing him, as he had threatened to do.

The Marquis knew that there was no need for the Earl himself to go to the Queen and complain about his behaviour.

He had only to relate what had happened to his friend, Lord Toddington, a Lord-in-Waiting, who was known as the 'arch-gossip of all gossips'.

He was, in fact, noted as being a danger both inside the Palace and out, for he repeated everything he heard either to the Prince Consort or to the Queen herself.

'Dammit!' the Marquis thought as he read the letter, 'I bet this is Toddington's doing!'

He was aware that his plans for leaving for the country would have to be postponed.

As he dressed himself appropriately for a visit to Buckingham Palace, he thought he would undoubtedly feel like a schoolboy being given a 'ticking off' by the Headmaster.

The Queen had made it quite clear, doubtless at the instigation of the Prince Consort, that she would not have any more duelling, though the ban had incurred quite an amount of criticism.

Duelling had been the gentlemanly way of settling an argument that had been accepted most amicably by George IV and tolerated by his successor.

Few duellists were actually killed, but if one was, it was customary for his opponent to disappear for several months to the Continent.

The whole episode was then conveniently forgotten, except by those who mourned the dead.

The Marquis was far too good a shot to do anything more than just wing his opponent in the arm.

Then, as the referee would consider honour was satisfied, the duel came to an end.

'I might have thought,' the Marquis told himself, 'that Castleton was the vengeful sort and determined to have his 'pound of flesh', one way or the other."

Because he felt defiant, not only in respect of what the Earl had done, but also because the Queen had become involved in it, he deliberately drove himself to Buckingham Palace.

It was considered correct for gentlemen calling there to arrive in a closed carriage.

The Marquis however swept in through the iron gates with their two sentries on guard, driving a pair of superb, perfectly matched horses, drawing a chaise that had only recently been delivered by the coach builders.

He drew his horses to a standstill under the pillared entrance to the State Rooms, handed the reins to his groom and walked in with an air which made the flunkeys in their Royal livery regard him with admiration.

They all followed his victories on the turf and often had a flutter on his horses, which invariably won.

As the Marquis walked up the red-carpeted stairs, one footman said to the other,

"I wish I'd had the nerve to ask 'im what 'e's running at Ascot and get a good price!"

"Bet you won't do that!" the other one replied with a grin.

The Marquis was escorted along the wide passage on the first floor towards the Queen's private apartments.

They overlooked the garden at the back of the Palace and he saw, when he was announced and entered, that the sunshine was enveloping the room with a golden haze.

As he approached the Queen at the far end, he was aware she was looking stern and unsmiling, and he knew he was in for an uncomfortable interview.

Actually, the Queen had always liked handsome men from the time of her accession, when she had adored the handsome, raffish Lord Melbourne.

She was thinking now, as the Marquis walked towards her, that it would be difficult to find a better-looking man in the whole of the Court Circle.

The way the Marquis's hair grew back from his square forehead, his finely cut features which betokened his aristocratic breeding and his athletic body, without an ounce of superfluous flesh on it, would have made him outstanding anywhere in the world.

The Queen, even if she was unaware of it, was beguiled like every other woman by the fact the Marquis appeared to regard life with a cynical amusement which set him apart from ordinary people.

It showed not only in the expression of his eyes but in the cynicism expressed by his firm, almost cruel lips, and the way he often drawled his words, as if he were completely indifferent as to whether anybody was interested in what he had to say or not.

Above all, he had a presence the Queen recognised as something she had always admired in a man.

She liked men who were strong, not only physically but mentally, who wished to dominate and master those around them and who, whether they knew it or not, had the magnetism of a leader.

She noticed all this in the Marquis, as he bowed his head respectfully in front of her.

However, she remembered as he did so, that he had behaved abominably, which was something she would not tolerate in those she considered part of her intimate circle.

"Good morning, Marquis!" she said in her rather high voice, which had lost its girlish gaiety in the years she had been married and produced so many children.

"Good morning, Ma'am."

"The Prince Consort and I have a special duty to entrust to you."

This was not at all what the Marquis had expected, and he looked at the Queen a little wanly before he replied.

"I am very honoured, Ma'am."

"We wish you," the Queen went on, "to represent us at the wedding of Prince Fredrick of Bãlutik and Lady Clotilda Tevington-Hyde."

For a moment the Marquis looked puzzled.

"Bãlutik, Ma'am?"

"I presume you know where it is?" the Queen said sharply.

"Unless I am mistaken, Ma'am," the Marquis murmured, "it is a Balkan country to the south of Serbia."

"You are quite right," the Queen agreed, "and the Prince Consort and I have just arranged that the reigning Prince, who is very distantly related to the Saxe-Coburgs, should be married to my Goddaughter, whose father was the late Duke of Hyde."

There was a little silence as the Marquis digested this, trying frantically to remember what he knew of Bãlutik and its Monarch.

"Prince Frederick is eager to be married in a month's time," the Queen went on, "which means, Marquis, that you will have to leave almost immediately and escort Lady Clotilda first by sea, then by carriage to the Capital."

"Escort Lady Clotilda, Ma'am?"

"Yes, Marquis, that is what the Prince Consort and I have arranged, because unfortunately the present Duke of Hyde, who is an elderly cousin and her guardian, is not well enough to undertake the journey. He is, poor man, crippled with rheumatoid arthritis, and of course the Duchess cannot leave him."

The Marquis drew in his breath to say that he did not think he was a suitable escort for a young bride, but the Queen went on.

"It will of course take you out of London for the rest of the Season, but I think you will agree, Marquis, that is perhaps a good thing in the circumstances – of which we will not speak!"

The Marquis, feeling that no answer was required, merely bowed his head slightly and the Queen went on.

"I am afraid you will find it a somewhat arduous journey, but Prince Fredrick is sending a warship to convey his future bride. I think it is, in fact, the only one that Bãlutik possesses, but once you reach the nearest port, everything will be arranged, I am sure, for your comfort and convenience."

As the Queen finished speaking, the Marquis knew that his punishment for being involved in the duel had been thought out very competently and, he was quite certain, by the Prince Consort.

The only thing he could do in the circumstances therefore was to accept the inevitable and at the same time, if only to save his pride, make it appear that he found it a pleasant duty and was not the least humiliated by it.

"I can only thank you, Ma'am," he said slowly but with what seemed to be a note of sincerity in his voice, "for offering me a duty that I shall find of the utmost interest. I have in fact always longed to visit some of the Balkan countries and will certainly avail myself of the opportunity after I have delivered the bride to her prospective bridegroom."

Watching the Queen, he thought her somewhat protruding eyes looked surprised at the way he had spoken.

He knew that what he had said would be related to the Prince Consort immediately after his departure.

"The Minster for Bãlutik will call on you, Marquis, with every detail later this afternoon," the Queen said, "and I know that he will wish you to leave these shores by Saturday at the very latest."

"I am certain that can be arranged, Ma'am," the Marquis replied, "and thank you once again for entrusting me with such a pleasant duty and the great honour of representing both Your Majesty and the Prince Consort."

As the Queen appeared to have nothing more to say, he bowed and backed out of her presence.

Outside the door he found waiting for him not the Major Domo who had escorted him to the Royal apartments, but Lord Toddington, who he was quite certain was responsible for what had just occurred.

Lord Toddington had on his face what the Marquis thought was the odious expression of somebody who thinks he has just brought off a brilliant coup and is longing to tittle-tattle about it to anybody with whom he comes in contact.

They shook hands and as the Marquis walked down the corridor with Lord Toddington beside him, he said,

"It is a very interesting idea, and I look to you, Toddington, to tell me everything you know about Bãlutik. I am sure you are a mine of information about it!"

It was an invitation Lord Toddington could not resist.

"You did not meet Prince Fredrick when he was here about five years ago?" he asked.

"If I did, I cannot remember him," the Marquis replied. "How old is he?"

"He is forty-nine."

The Marquis looked surprised.

"A bridegroom?"

"Second marriage," Lord Toddington said. "His wife died two years ago, and he wishes to ally himself more closely to the English Crown."

"Her Majesty said he was distantly related to the Prince Consort."

"Very, very distantly," Lord Toddington answered, "but he makes the most of it."

"What is he like?" the Marquis enquired. "Confidentially, of course!"

Lord Toddington glanced over his shoulder as if he thought somebody might be listening.

"Completely humourless and puffed up with his own importance! But he is determined to make Bãlutik a model state on the German pattern."

The Marquis laughed.

"One day, Toddington, you will have to write a book. It will be a bestseller!"

"I have often thought of it," Lord Toddington said. "If it were not for the fear that if I described truthfully everybody who came to the Palace, I should be exiled for years, if not for life!"

He gave the Marquis a sideways glance as he spoke, who knew exactly what he was thinking.

"Fill me in with more details," the Marquis said, "so that I shall not make any mistakes when I represent Her Majesty and the Prince Consort at the wedding."

Lord Toddington stopped at the top of the stairs that led down to the hall.

He lowered his voice as he said,

"If you want to please the Prince, take him some dirty postcards, such as can be bought in Leicester Square, or Charing Cross Road."

The Marquis looked at Lord Toddington in astonishment.

"Dirty postcards?" he asked beneath his breath.

"Actually, we had a hell of a time with him when he was here," Lord Toddington went on. "All he wanted was to be taken to the lowest and most erotic haunts of London nightlife! You know what I mean by nightlife?"

The Marquis did not answer, and Lord Toddington went on.

"I do not mind telling you, it was a bit of an eye-opener to me. Personally, I have never been interested in that sort of thing, but the Prince wanted to sample the very dregs!"

"Sounds rather depraved to me!" the Marquis said dryly.

"He was!" Lord Toddington agreed. "And as I do not find it amusing to witness a very young girl being either ravished or whipped, I preferred to wait in the carriage outside until he had had enough!"

"If what you are saying is true, it sounds to me as if His Royal Highness is a complete 'outsider'," the Marquis said slowly. "Have you told the Queen what he is like?".

"No, of course not!" Lord Toddington said in a shocked voice. "She would not want to believe that any relation of Prince Albert's, however distant, could be anything but perfect and, of course, exactly like him?"

"Albert the Good!" the Marquis said beneath his breath, and Lord Toddington laughed.

They walked down the stairs into the hall and although Lord Toddington looked slightly surprised when the Marquis's chaise was brought to the door, he said nothing.

The Marquis stepped into the driving seat and picked up the reins.

As he raised his whip in a salute and drove off, Lord Toddington, going back into the Palace, said to himself,

'The Marquis of Weybourne is always full of surprises. I really believe he is looking forward to going to Bãlutik!'

It was certainly not what he had expected, and he wondered if he should remark upon it to the Queen.

*

The Marquis, driving back to Park Lane, thought with a cynical smile that he had undoubtedly surprised both the Queen and Lord Toddington.

It meant however that he would miss Royal Ascot, at which he had intended to be a considerable winner and it was doubtful if he would be back in time for Goodwood.

'*Curse it*, but I believe I hoodwinked them!' he said to himself.

Only as he drew up outside his house in Park Lane did he remember that while he had asked for information about the bridegroom, he had not mentioned the bride and, for that matter, neither had Lord Toddington.

CHAPTER TWO

Lady Clotilda rode into the stable yard and dismounting, patted her horse's neck affectionately.

As she did so an old groom came slowly out of one of the stables to ask,

"'Ad a good ride, Me Lady?"

"Marvellous, thank you, Abbey! I have never known Swallow to jump better!"

"E'll 'ave to be careful on the 'igh jumps," the old man said "E'll 'ave a nasty fall if he ain't careful?"

"I will be careful," Lady Clotilda smiled.

She patted her horse's neck again and turned away, conscious as she did so that she was late, and her aunt would be annoyed.

As she had rode, it had been difficult to think of anything but the joy of being out in the sunshine and free of the gloom which had seemed to envelop Hyde Castle like a fog, ever since her father's death.

Before, it had seemed to her they were always laughing, and despite the fact that her father had the greatest difficulty in what he called 'making two ends meet', he could always joke about it.

It had come as a complete surprise to him when he had come into the Dukedom.

There were two brothers, both older than him, and it had never entered his mind that he might, one day, take his father's place.

Lord Julian Tevington-Hyde, as he then was, had therefore made the best of the extremely small allowance, which was all he had to live on, by travelling what was called 'rough'.

He had seen the world in a very different way from those who could afford to travel in the best ships and stay in the most comfortable hotels or, where people of importance were concerned, in the best homes or Palaces.

Lord Julian had however enjoyed life much more than most of his contemporaries did and as he was extremely proficient in languages, he got to know the natives of the countries he visited, as few Englishmen were able to do.

This was because his grandmother had been a Balkan Princess and she had talked to him in her own language when he was small.

This had instilled in him a desire to learn other languages, which indeed he continued to acquire all his life.

Clotilda had found it fascinating to listen to the tales her father told of his travels and later, when he became a widower, actually to travel with him herself.

They visited various places in Africa and in Europe that were certainly not in the accepted curriculum of other girls of her social standing.

"It would be different if you had a son, Julian," his relatives would remonstrate with him, "but to take Clotilda with you is quite absurd and will certainly spoil her chances of making a good marriage when she is a debutante."

Lord Julian had laughed.

"I should have thought it would increase her chances of keeping her husband amused and would prevent him from wandering off to look for somebody else more entertaining."

This reply shocked his relatives all the more. They ceased to argue with him and merely said amongst themselves that Julian had no sense of responsibility and ignored him.

This however they were unable to do once he became the Duke of Hyde.

It seemed an extraordinary coincidence that his two elder brothers should have died within a few months of each other and for quite different reasons.

Henry, the elder of the two, was killed fighting in India while John, the next brother, who was in the same Regiment, contracted yellow fever on his way home and died in Cape Town.

Their deaths came to Julian like a bombshell, so did they to the rest of the family.

"Julian, the Duke? I have never heard of such a thing!" they exclaimed.

Yet strangely enough in a short time he undertook his responsibilities as head of a very large and diverse family, and he became a very good one.

This certainly did not surprise Clotilda, who had always known that her father's sympathy and understanding of all sorts and conditions of people made him an excellent judge of character and a compassionate landlord.

Unfortunately, he could not always translate this into action by providing the money that was vitally needed by the farmers, the tenants, the pensioners and everybody else on the Hyde estate.

The money was just not there.

Although, in the teeth of opposition from any of the family who knew about it, the new Duke had sold quite a number of items of value in the Castle, they were still hard up and found it more and more difficult to keep up appearances.

This had not affected Clotilda, but when she was eighteen and should have been a debutante and presented at Court, her father had a fatal riding accident, and she was in deep mourning.

It seemed incredible that a man who was so experienced at riding anything from an elephant to a yak should kill himself accidentally jumping over a hedge he had cleared a dozen times before.

And yet when he had fallen the Duke had cracked his spine and the only consolation to Clotilda when he died was that if he had lived he would have been completely paralysed.

'Papa would have hated that!' she told herself.

The moment the Duke was dead, another Duke came to take his place.

This was in the person of a cousin whom nobody had ever liked. He was an elderly man, disagreeable by nature, and even more so because he was stricken with an acute form of rheumatoid arthritis that kept him in a wheelchair.

He was in fact disagreeable from first thing in the morning until last thing at night and made his wife's life a misery, which resulted in her being extremely disagreeable too.

To Clotilda it was such a change from the happiness she had known, first with her mother and father together, then with her father alone, that she could hardly believe it.

As the days seemed filled with darkness, complaints and endless rows over small, unimportant trifles, her only escape was to ride Swallow and remember the past.

Her father had given her Swallow when he was just a foal and because Clotilda had always looked after him herself, he followed her wherever she went and came when she called him.

He had turned into a very fine horse and an excellent jumper, and she was sure that if she entered him in the local point-to-point next year, he would be a winner.

She had not done so before for the simple reason that she had thought it seemed wrong when she was still in mourning for her father.

But she had many plans for herself and Swallow, and she was thinking of him now as she walked in through the side door and up some uncarpeted stairs that led to the centre of the Castle.

It was only as she reached the hall that she saw through the open front door a very impressive carriage standing outside, drawn by four horses.

It was unusual for anybody to be calling at the Castle in the morning, and she stared at the carriage wondering who could have come to see her uncle, and if they would be staying for luncheon.

Then as she was about to ascend the stairs to her bedroom her aunt came from the Morning Room that was always used when they were alone to say sharply,

"Oh, there you are, Clotilda! You are late, as usual!"

"I am sorry, Aunt Augusta," Clotilda replied, "but it is such a lovely day that I am afraid I forgot the time."

The Duchess came towards her saying,

"Well, hurry and change your clothes, and be quick about it. It is very important!"

Clotilda, who had reached the first steps of the staircase, looked at her in surprise.

"Important?" she questioned "Why?"

"You will hear that as soon as you are changed, so do as I say, and hurry!"

There was an urgency in the Duchess's voice which made Clotilda's eyes widen.

Obediently she ran up the stairs and from there to the end of the corridor where her bedroom was situated.

Because the castle was far too big, when her father inherited, he decided that they themselves should use all the best rooms on the first floor rather than keep them for distinguished guests.

The second floor was therefore to all intents and purposes closed and the servants used the floor above that.

As there were not many of them, a great many of those bedrooms were closed too.

Clotilda entered what had always been known as Charles II's Room, although it was very doubtful if he had ever stayed in the Castle and began to take off her riding habit.

It was worn and rather shabby and she had in fact in the last two years grown out of it, but there was little likelihood of her having another one.

Therefore, despite the haste she was in, she hung it up in the wardrobe before she changed into a plain cotton gown that had been made for her by a seamstress who came to the Castle two days a week.

She was paid only a pittance for her sewing, though Clotilda often thought she was worth her weight in gold, for without Mrs Geery it was doubtful if she would ever have had anything respectable to wear.

She buttoned her gown and crossed the room to her dressing table to look at her reflection in the mirror.

It was a very pretty, in fact lovely face that looked back at her, with large eyes fringed with dark lashes, which was surprising, considering her hair was very fair.

"You have your great-grandmother's eyes, Dearest," her father had said once, "who was considered a great beauty in Romania, but you have the fair hair of the Hydes, which came originally from some Viking ancestor. I have always meant to look him up in the family tree."

Clotilda had laughed.

"I am quite happy to have hair the same colour as yours, Papa."

"What it all boils down to," her father had said, "is that I have a very pretty daughter and I love her very much."

"As I love you," Clotilda had replied. "And nobody in the whole world has a more adventurous, exciting and linguistic Papa, of that I am sure!"

They both laughed and to prove her point, Clotilda had chatted away to him in Arabic while he had answered her in Turkish.

Now her hair seemed to have caught the sunshine as she tidied it in the mirror, thinking as she did so there was not time to rearrange it in an elaborate fashion.

She therefore twisted it into a knot at the back of her head.

She was aware it was fashionable to have ringlets but she never seemed to have the time to arrange them, and even if she had, who would notice?.

Her uncle usually looked at her with dislike and she was well aware he considered her an encumbrance as a relative to whom he had to offer his hospitality because there was nowhere else for her to go.

Clotilda had actually racked her brain after her father's death to think of any relations with whom she could live rather than stay at the Castle.

But nobody had offered to take her into their homes and she had no wish to go anywhere unless she could take Swallow with her.

It was however very humiliating to know that both her uncle and aunt thought of her as a 'cross they must bear', a duty to be undertaken unwillingly.

Clotilda turned away from the dressing table and hurried down the stairs knowing that however quick she was, her aunt would think it was not quick enough.

She noted as she crossed the hall that the carriage was still outside. She entered the drawing room to find the visitor was a strange and rather distinguished-looking man with grey hair who looked at her, she thought, so intently that she felt it was almost an insult.

"There you are, Clotilda!" her uncle, who was sitting in his wheelchair by the fireplace, remarked.

"Yes, I am here, Uncle Edward," Clotilda replied, "and I am sorry if I have kept you waiting."

"We have a visitor," the Duke said ponderously. "Your Excellency, this is the daughter of my predecessor, Lady Clotilda Tevington-Hyde."

Clotilda curtsied and held out her hand, but to her surprise the gentleman bowed and raised it in foreign fashion perfunctorily to his lips.

"It is a great honour, and an inexpressible delight to meet you, Lady Clotilda," he said.

The way he spoke was somewhat surprising. Then the Duke said,

"His Excellency has come here with Her Majesty the Queen's approval to bring you a proposal of marriage from Crown Prince Fredrick of Bãlutik?"

The Duke spoke slowly and ponderously, but for a moment Clotilda felt that what she was hearing could not be true and that she must be dreaming.

"Wh-what did you say, Uncle Edward?"

"I should have thought it was quite clear," the Duchess joined in sharply. "His Royal Highness wishes you, although it seems extraordinary, to be his wife!"

"It cannot be possible!" Clotilda cried "I am not Royal!"

The Minister smiled.

"You have forgotten, My Lady, that your great-grandmother was the Princess Marie-Celeste of Romania."

"Yes of course," Clotilda agreed, "but I should not have thought it was enough."

"Quite enough to ensure that His Royal Highness will be more than delighted that the Queen has given her approval to your marriage. Now there is nothing to prevent the arrangements, which have been made some time ago, from going ahead."

"What arrangements? I do not – understand," Clotilda said in a bewildered voice.

Because she suddenly felt weak and a little frightened, she sat down on a sofa and the Minister moving nearer to her said,

"I think I should explain to you that His Royal Highness is extremely eager that Bãlutik should show its great respect and affection for the British Crown."

Clotilda was well aware that this could be said of a great many small countries in Europe who wished to retain their independence.

"As His Royal Highness is very proud to be related to the Prince Consort," the Minister went on, "he approached Her Majesty Queen Victoria and suggested that he should marry an Englishwoman to share with her the throne of Bãlutik."

"H-he could not have heard of me!" Clotilda said in a small voice.

"I think you underrate our efficiency in Bãlutik," the Minister answered, "and as I represent my country in London, I was able, knowing you to be a Goddaughter of the Queen, to put your name forward for her approval."

Clotilda had the idea there had been several other names on the list as well, but she was too diplomatic to say so even though she felt dazed and still bewildered by what had been said.

"Now everything is settled," the Minister said with what she thought was a note of relief in his voice. "The only thing that may seem a little troublesome is that His Royal Highness wishes you to leave by the end of next week."

"By the end of next week?" the Duchess repeated. "But that is impossible!"

"Nothing is impossible, Your Grace," the Minister said with a smile, "and I assure you that His Royal Highness has thought out every detail so that there should be no unnecessary discomfort."

"I call it unnecessary and very uncomfortable for any bride to be married in such a short time?"

The Minister threw out his hands in an expressive gesture.

"I do understand your feelings, Your Grace," he said. "At the same time, His Royal Highness is eager for a summer wedding and at a time when a great number of his subjects will be visiting the Capital, to delay any longer would mean that the weather would be far too hot and the date inconveniently close to harvest time."

"I understand what you are saying," the Duke said testily, "and Clotilda must make the effort to be ready."

"Are you saying," Clotilda asked in a very small voice, "that I shall not meet Prince Fredrick until I arrive in Bãlutik?"

"I am afraid it is impossible for him to come to England at this particular moment," the Minister answered, "but His Royal Highness is doing everything in his power to make you happy."

His voice became ingratiatingly slower.

"There will be a battleship to convey you and your party to Drina, which is the nearest port, and from there you will be escorted by the military through Albania into Bãlutik. It is quite a short journey and will involve your having to stay for only one night on the way."

"I suppose," the Duchess interposed before Clotilda could speak, "His Royal Highness has forgotten that a bride needs a trousseau?"

The Minister smiled.

"That is where you are wrong, Your Grace, if you will forgive my saying so, His Royal Highness, because of the speed at which everything needs to be done, has empowered me to order what is necessary from the best and most important dressmakers in London."

"Are you saying," Clotilda asked, "that you have already bought my trousseau?"

"I admit I consulted my wife, who is extremely knowledgeable in such matters," the Minister replied, "and since the gowns may require some small alteration, My Lady, I have arranged for the dressmakers to call here at the Castle tomorrow morning."

He looked at the Duke before he continued.

"I am hoping, as there is much to do, that His Grace will be kind enough to offer them his hospitality for two or three nights. They will also bring with them most of the other things you will require."

He paused to look with satisfaction at the astonished faces of his audience before he went on.

"Anything that is not ready for Saturday week can of course come later. My wife assures me that there will in fact be a great number of trunks to be taken aboard our warship."

"I cannot believe it!" the Duchess exclaimed. "Quite frankly, Count, if you want my opinion, I think such haste is quite unsuitable, and for the bridegroom to provide the bride's trousseau is almost an insult."

"Perhaps, Your Grace, I should let you into a little secret," the Minister said. "Her Majesty the Queen could not make up her mind as swiftly as we have wished. In fact, for the last four weeks, I have called every day at the Palace hoping for a favourable reply to His Royal Highness's request."

There was a note in his voice that told Clotilda he had in fact been very worried.

Then with a smile he finished by saying,

"Yesterday, to my delight, the Queen's answer was in the affirmative and I was able to go ahead with the arrangements."

"I feel we should have been given far more warning than this!" the Duchess sniffed.

"I can only apologise," the Minister said humbly, "but I promise you, I did everything I could."

There was a silence, then Clotilda said,

"Supposing I do not accept His Royal Highness's proposal?"

Her voice was very faint, but there was no doubt that all three people listening heard what she had said.

There was a look of consternation on the Minister's face, and he was very still, as if turned to stone.

The Duchess merely looked at Clotilda, while the Duke, who seemed to recover his senses more quickly than the others, said sharply,

"What do you mean – not accept?. Of course you will accept. It is not only a great honour to you, but to the family. Perhaps I should have said before that on behalf of myself and those of my blood, we consider it an honour, and there is no other word for it."

"But I have never seen His Royal Highness," Clotilda said faintly.

"What has that to do with it?" the Duke asked testily. "Once you are married you will have plenty of time to get to know him."

Because he thought the Duke was taking the wrong attitude, the Minister moved a little closer to Clotilda and said in a low voice,

"I assure you, Lady Clotilda, that everybody in Bãlutik, from our reigning Monarch down to his lowliest subject, will welcome you and do everything in their power to make you happy."

He was watching her eyes as he spoke and feeling she was unconvinced he said,

"Bãlutik is a very beautiful country. It has high mountains and the rivers that run through it make it extremely fertile."

He looked at her again, and feeling she was still uncertain he said,

"You may at first find the language a little difficult. It is rather more Serbian than Hungarian, but there is an undoubted resemblance in many ways to Romanian."

"I speak both Romanian and Serbian," Clotilda said.

"You do?"

The Minister sounded incredulous. Then he said,

"But of course! I did hear that your father was extremely proficient in languages, but it was something I was remiss enough to forget."

"I do not believe Papa ever went to Bãlutik," Clotilda said slowly.

"But he visited many other countries in the Balkans."

As the Minister spoke, Clotilda was rather doubtful if this was true.

"Papa travelled all over the world," she said, "and, of course, my mother could speak Romanian and many other Balkan languages."

"Of that I am sure," the Minister said, "and that is why I know, Lady Clotilda, that both your father and mother would be very proud to think of you reigning over Bãlutik and bringing an English influence to our lovely land."

He was trying to coax her into seeing the advantages of the position she would hold, Clotilda thought.

But every instinct in her body told her that she should not be pushed into doing something that was not only frightening, but was, she thought, wrong because it entailed marriage to a man she had never seen.

Almost as if he read her thoughts the Minister said,

"I have brought with me, My Lady, a portrait of His Royal Highness. It is in my carriage, and I thought I would leave it for you."

There was nothing Clotilda could do but murmur, "Thank you," and the Minister turned to the Duke,

"What I would like to suggest, Your Grace, for your approval, is that when the dressmakers come here tomorrow my wife comes with them, and also brings the Lady-in-Waiting who is to accompany Lady Clotilda on her journey to Bãlutik."

"Surely she is to have an English Lady-in-Waiting with her?" the Duchess enquired.

The Minister shook his head.

"His Royal Highness thought, and I think wisely, that it would be a mistake for Lady Clotilda not to be accompanied by a Lady-in-Waiting from our own country. A lady's maid also will arrive tomorrow. She is waiting in my ministry in London. A pleasant woman, well up in her duties, and with impeccable references from other ladies she has served in the past."

"It seems to me a very strange way of conducting things," the Duchess said. "I presume that both you and His Royal Highness realised that my husband is not well enough to undertake such a long journey, and I cannot leave him alone. But I should have thought that Clotilda should have some English person with her to help and guide her until she is actually married."

As if he were playing a trump card the Minister replied,

"Her Majesty has already thought of that, Your Grace, and she had appointed the Marquis of Weybourne to represent herself and the Prince Consort at the wedding, and to accompany Lady Clotilda on the journey."

"The Marquis of Weybourne?" the Duchess exclaimed. "A most unsuitable choice."

"It was Her Majesty who suggested it, Your Grace."

The Duchess pressed her thin lips together and looked at the Duke.

"Weybourne? He has some excellent horses," the Duke remarked. "Won the Derby this year?"

"We are speaking of Clotilda, Edward?"

"I know! I know!" the Duke said testily. "But we cannot interfere, my dear, with the Queen's choice of who is to represent her at the wedding."

"No, of course not," the Duchess agreed, "but 1 still think she should have an English lady at her side."

"I think when you meet the Baroness who is to accompany her and is, in fact, the widow of one of our most distinguished diplomats, you will realise that nobody could be a better support and mentor in such unusual circumstances," the Minister said.

The Duchess sniffed, but she did not say anything.

As if she felt she could not bear any more, Clotilda rose to her feet.

She walked across the room to stand at the open window looking out into the untidy garden for which there were never enough gardeners to keep it looking anything but wild and overgrown.

She was not for the moment thinking of how frightening it would be to be married to a man she had never met or to live in a strange country about which she knew very little.

Instead, she was thinking that she must leave Swallow behind, and how agonising it would be to part with him.

'I cannot do it,' she said to herself.

Then almost as if he were standing beside her, she saw her father smiling at her, the little twinkle in his eye that was always there when anything amused him or he was setting out on some sort of adventure.

'How can I refuse, Papa?' she asked him in her heart.

Then as if she could hear him answer she knew he was telling her that she had very little choice except to leave Swallow behind.

So often in the long nights these last two years when she had not been able to sleep she had talked to him and told him how much she missed him and how bleak and dismal the Castle was.

Nothing ever happened there except frequent outbursts of bad temper from her uncle.

'Go! Go!' she felt her father was saying to her. 'The world is a big place and anything is better than living here in misery.'

It was what she had thought for some time, but she had never felt her father was so near to her or so positive in answering her call to him.

She turned from the window, realising that all the time she had stood there, there had been silence behind her.

Then with a smile, which she brought to her lips with an almost superhuman effort, she said,

"I shall look forward, Your Excellency, to meeting your wife tomorrow and thanking her for all the trouble she has taken over my trousseau."

*

Driving down to Tilbury, the Marquis knew he was behaving unconventionally and certainly rather rudely in refusing to drive, as the Minister had assumed he would, with the carriages of the bride and her entourage.

"If there is one thing I dislike, Your Excellency," he had said loftily, "it is being shut up in a closed carriage either alone or with some strange woman who will doubtless consider it correct to weep copiously because she is saying goodbye to her home."

"I had hoped," the Minister said simply, "that Your Lordship would meet Lady Clotilda at the Ministry before we set out, and of course both my wife and I will come to Tilbury to see the ship leave."

He added as if to make it sound more attractive, "we will also be accompanied by Ministers and Ambassadors from other Balkan countries who wish to pay their respects to the future wife of His Royal Highness."

"Quite right!" the Marquis approved. "And I shall have plenty of time to say all the things that have been left unsaid during what I am certain will be an uncomfortable passage through the Bay of Biscay."

"I hope not," the Minister replied, "but of course the weather in the Bay is always unpredictable."

"Like most women!" the Marquis said cynically.

He was thinking as he spoke of what a commotion it had caused when he had told Hester he was going abroad.

He had known that as far as he was concerned it was an easy way of ending their association, far easier than he had expected.

Hester had tried to cling to him and tell him she would die a thousand deaths in the months he would be away, and had sworn eternal fidelity, expecting him to do the same.

The Marquis fortunately could spend only a little time with her owing to the fact that Sir Anthony was in London.

What made things more difficult was that the Countess of Castleton, hearing he was leaving London, had risked her reputation and her husband's wrath by calling to see the Marquis surreptitiously.

He had arrived back at his house in Grosvenor Square to be told there was a lady waiting to see him, and he had thought the only person indiscreet enough to come to his house would be Hester.

To his complete astonishment when he entered the library it was to find Sheila Castleton, swathed in veils and looking, he had to admit, extremely lovely.

"I had to come!" she said before he could speak. "I *had to*, Stanwin!"

She moved close against him as she said,

"I know it is all my fault that you are being sent away to some outlandish place."

"How do you know that?" the Marquis asked.

"Arthur was boasting that he was instrumental in getting you sent there, for he knew the Queen would be angry if she heard about your duel."

"As it happens, I am looking forward to visiting Bãlutik?"

"And leaving me? Oh, Stanwin, how can you say such a thing?" Sheila Castleton protested.

He wanted to say there was nothing else he could do in the circumstances. At the same time, it was an opportunity he welcomed.

He still had no intention of letting anybody guess how angry he was at being punished like a small child.

He was determined that his friends should not pity him and had made light of the fact when he was in the club that he was going to miss Royal Ascot.

"I thought you were going to win the Gold Cup, Weybourne," the Earl of Derby said to him.

"I think I am!" the Marquis replied.

"Do you mean to say you are still running your horses even though you will not be there?"

"Why not? It is just unfortunate that two such pleasant events should clash, but I do not expect the races, or the Royal Enclosure will be any different from what they were last year and will be next!"

"I cannot understand it!" the Marquis's friends said amongst themselves. "It almost seems as if he welcomes the opportunity of going abroad in the middle of the Season."

Only Harry knew the truth.

"You are putting a good face on it, Stanwin," he said, "and I think most people have been deceived. At the same time I am *damned* sorry for you."

"If you want the truth, I am *damned* sorry for myself," the Marquis replied. "But I have no intention of giving Her Majesty or anybody else the satisfaction of thinking I have submitted to punishment."

"No, of course not," Harry agreed, "and I will keep up the illusion that you are jumping over the moon with joy at having the privilege of escorting some unfledged, boring bride to her doom?"

"For God's sake," the Marquis said, "do not rub it in. If we were travelling in a British ship, it would be some consolation. But I do not speak their blasted language and have no intention of trying."

"You speak German," Harry replied, "and I do not mind betting you the officers will be German."

The Marquis laughed.

"I expect you are right, in which case I am sorry for the poor devils under them!"

"You will doubtless also find yourself sympathising with the bride," Harry said. "I have heard some very unpleasant things about Prince Fredrick."

"So have I," the Marquis agreed, "but I am sure that to her, like all women, all that matters is the chance of wearing a crown?"

He spoke with a bitterness that made Harry remember why the Marquis had never married.

It was something that was known perhaps only to him and, despite the fact that they were close friends, it was something they never discussed.

The Marquis had been twenty-one when he first fell seriously in love, and as his father was the younger son there was no likelihood of his inheriting the title.

The girl to whom he had lost his heart was the Beauty of the Season, an exquisite creature who had a great many eligible young men at her feet, but none so handsome or so attractive as Stanwin Bourne.

He had kissed her for the first time in the garden when they were attending a ball at Devonshire House.

After that they met secretly almost every day and danced with each other openly every night at balls to which they were both invited.

When Stanwin asked her to marry him she had agreed to a secret understanding, saying her mother would think she was too young to be married in her first Season.

Then as Stanwin walked about with his head in the clouds he had, just before the parties ended and everybody left London for the country, been told by the girl he loved that she was going to marry somebody else.

"I am sorry, Stanwin," she said, "and you know I love you! I do not think I shall ever love anyone as much. But Hugh is an Earl, and I shall be a hereditary Lady-in-Waiting to the Queen."

"Are you telling me," Stanwin asked in a voice that did not sound like his own, "that you are marrying him just because of that?"

"It is everything I have ever wanted, and Mama and Papa are so pleased. And he has such a wonderful house and estate in Buckinghamshire."

It was three years before the Marquis's father unexpectedly inherited the title and the vast estates, which should in fact have gone to his elder brother.

Then two years after that Stanwin, who had lost his first and only real love because his prospects were not good enough for her, became the Marquis of Weybourne.

There was no other aristocrat in the country who owned so much land, and there was nobody who looked finer or more noble when he appeared at Court.

It was however some satisfaction to him to realise that since the marriage, the Earl who had supplanted him had grown plump and bald and his wife, while still beautiful, had a discontented droop to her lips.

Also, despite the fact that they already had three daughters, there was as yet no son and heir.

The Marquis missed nothing, but also said nothing.

It was only to Harry, because they were so close, that the Marquis said he was convinced that women, while professing love, would sell themselves for a social position and the highest title obtainable.

"You have to marry one day," Harry had said to the Marquis once.

"There will be no difficulty about that," the Marquis replied, and Harry noticed the cynicism in his voice and the hardness of his expression.

There was no need for the Marquis to elaborate the fact that he was sure that any young woman would willingly accept him for his possessions and his title alone, and it would be quite unnecessary to have his heart thrown in.

'Perhaps one day he will fall in love again,' Harry mused to himself.

At the same time, he had the uncomfortable feeling it was unlikely.

Driving towards Tilbury, the Marquis thought for the first time, remembering what Toddington had said to him, and having received confirmation in further detail from some of the members of *White's*, that the bride was in for a hard time.

'What will it matter,' he asked himself, 'when the daughter of a dead Duke has jumped into the position of a reigning Princess?'

As his horses gave him a little trouble he added,

'Let us hope she has spirit enough to stand up to him.'

Then he remembered that the Prince was a German and thought it was unlikely he would listen to anybody, let alone his wife.

CHAPTER THREE

All the way to Tilbury, Clotilda felt as if she were going to her doom.

She was so astonished and bewildered when she was told that Prince Fredrick of Bãlutik wanted to marry her that she had agreed without making any further fuss.

Then after Countess Jãkicic, the Minister's wife, arrived with her trousseau she began to realise what her marriage would entail.

She would be virtually exiled to a strange land with a strange man whom she had never met, and the moment they were married would be the point of no return.

Because she was by now feeling very frightened, she said to her Aunt a few days before they were due to leave for Bãlutik,

"I suppose, Aunt Augusta, it is impossible now for me to say that I have changed my mind?"

The Duchess looked at her with what she thought was contempt.

"I suppose you are suffering from what is called 'Bridal Nerves'," she said scathingly "Well, forget them! Nobody is going to listen to you whining and complaining when, in my opinion, you are the most fortunate girl in the world?"

"I am not whining, Aunt Augusta. I am merely afraid of leaving you all and everything with which I am familiar. Supposing I am very unhappy? What shall I do?"

"You will be a reigning Princess, so make the best of it and behave like a courageous Englishwoman," the Duchess said firmly.

Then, with an unusual softness in her voice, she said,

"Of course, it is going to seem strange at first and marriage is difficult for any girl, however sophisticated and experienced in worldly matters she may be."

She paused and as Clotilda did not speak she went on,

"Just make up your mind that your husband is your master, and you have to obey him. He will doubtless do a lot of things that you will find extremely unpleasant, but that is a woman's lot, and there is nothing any of us can do about it?"

With that the Duchess walked out of the room, shutting the door somewhat noisily behind her.

Clotilda stared after her in bewilderment.

It was not what she had expected her aunt to say, and it made her even more apprehensive than she was already about the future.

She was of course thrilled with the beautiful clothes that the Countess, who was extremely smart herself, had bought for her in London.

The gowns were exactly what a young girl should wear, and her bridal gown was a dream of loveliness.

"Every woman in Bãlutik will be envious of you, my dear," the Countess said, "and there is nothing like beautiful clothes to give one confidence."

"That is certainly something I shall need," Clotilda said in a low voice.

The Countess seemed very understanding as she put her hand on Clotilda's arm and said,

"I know it must seem frightening having to do everything in such a hurry, but I assure you, my husband has been beseeching the Queen day after day to make a decision."

She gave a little laugh as she said,

"He has had a terrible time with letters arriving from Prince Frederick giving him orders that he could not carry out, and the Queen prevaricating so that he did not know whether he was on his head or his heels!"

The way she spoke was so funny that Clotilda smiled and said,

"I am sorry for being such a nuisance."

"Everything will be all right now! His Royal Highness will have his bride, and you will win every heart because you look so lovely!"

The Countess spoke with a sincerity that was unmistakable, and Clotilda said,

"I feel very remiss at not having thanked you properly for choosing such lovely clothes for me. At the same time, I feel it very wrong that His Royal Highness should pay for them."

"You should really thank my husband for that," the Countess replied. "He realised, as certainly nobody in Bãlutik could do, that your uncle is hard up and your father was able to leave you very little money when he died. He understood that being a Duke's daughter did not mean you were necessarily an heiress."

Clotilda laughed.

"That is certainly true! I could not have afforded even one of these lovely gowns, let alone so many of them?"

"That is what my husband thought," the Countess said with satisfaction. "He is a kind man, and he is actually very worried about you."

"Worried?" Clotilda asked.

The Countess looked away from her, which made Clotilda feel she had regretted what she had just said.

"He is worried in case you are not happy with all his arrangements," she said after a little pause, but Clotilda knew that was not what she had originally had in mind.

The portrait of Prince Fredrick that the Minister had left on his first visit was the usual picture of a Royal personage, Clotilda thought, in which the artist had taken far more trouble in portraying his decorations than his face.

Moreover, what she had always thought essential in a portrait was the character of the person and this had not been portrayed.

The portrait showed the head and shoulders of a man who seemed to be staring at something that annoyed him, and there appeared to be the beginning of a rebuke on his thick lips, which were set in a hard line.

His eyes protruded slightly and he looked young and, although German in appearance, good-looking.

The more she looked at the portrait, the more Clotilda felt instinctively that it was not a true picture of the man it portrayed.

She had felt this the first few days it had stood in her bedroom in the Castle, and then it was the Countess who gave her a clue to what she had known intuitively.

"How old is Prince Fredrick?" she asked casually when she was trying on her wedding gown.

Then before the Countess could reply she added,

"I suppose I should have asked this before."

There was a definite pause before the Countess replied.

"I suppose he must be going on forty-eight or forty-nine."

Clotilda gave a little gasp.

"Did you say forty-nine?"

"He may be a little younger than that, I am not sure," the Countess said quickly.

Clotilda knew then that the portrait that had been sent to her was a deception, a positive lie.

She was aware that the Prince had been married before and that his wife had died, but she had not imagined for one moment that he would be so old that he might easily be her father.

There was a long silence before finally she said,

"I should have thought His Royal Highness would have preferred to have somebody a little nearer his own age with whom he would have more things in common."

The Countess hesitated. Then she said,

"I believe all men, the older they get, like to think that a young wife will make them feel young again. Moreover, His Royal Highness wants an heir to the throne."

To Clotilda what she had now learnt made her more nervous and more frightened than she had been before.

She knew however that her aunt was right and there was nothing she could now do about it.

She felt instead that she was being swept along on a flood tide and every minute of every day enveloped her more tightly in chains that were unbreakable and from which she could never escape.

The Lady-in-Waiting, the Baroness von Kitzenstern, was very pleasant, a Dowager of the old school who had lived in many countries and had heard of her father.

"He was a great traveller," she said, "and I only wish I could have talked to him, I know we would have had many interesting experiences to share."

"One thing I want you to do, Baroness," Clotilda said, "is to talk to me in the language of my new country."

The Baroness looked surprised.

"It is not really necessary," she replied. "His Royal Highness insists that everybody in the Palace speaks German, which you can imagine is a severe handicap to our Statesmen, who are not always very good linguists."

Clotilda was not really surprised by this information.

She knew how insular the Germans were, and how they insisted on taking their language, their culture, their customs and their Army discipline with them wherever they went.

She had learned by this time that Bãlutik had offered the throne to Prince Fredrick fifteen years ago when, like many other Balkan countries, they were finding it difficult to provide a reigning King or Prince from their own people.

They had approached a Prince of the Danish Royal Family, who had refused, but Prince Fredrick, who was the youngest son of the ruler of a small principality, had accepted the position with alacrity.

Knowing how good-natured and easy-going many of the people of Balkan countries were, Clotilda could not help thinking it was a mistake for them to have a German ruling them.

But when she said this to the Baroness she replied quickly.

"His Royal Highness has done a great deal for Bãlutik. He has strengthened her defences, made her considerably more prosperous than she was before, and certainly made himself heard in the Council Chambers of Europe."

Clotilda wondered if this had made the people themselves any happier, but she did not like to ask awkward questions.

She was so certain the Baroness had been told to paint a very rosy picture of the country to which she was being taken so hurriedly that she felt she hardly had time to breathe, let alone think.

Although the Duchess complained at the way things were being done, Clotilda was aware that both she and the Duke were considerably impressed by the thoroughness with which the Prince and his Minister had thought out every detail, so as to spare them from having to exert themselves in any way concerning their niece's marriage.

They gave her as a wedding present a large and rather ugly diamond brooch, which was part of the Hyde collection, and assured her with a sincerity she could not doubt of how important she would be as Prince Fredrick's wife.

She also received quite a number of presents from her relations, many of whom had made no effort to communicate with her since her father died.

The presents were typical silver *entrée* dishes of which she was quite sure there would be any number at the Palace, crystal glass vases, which required very careful packing and were therefore an encumbrance, innumerable toast racks, leather-bound books and silver cigar boxes engraved with the names of the donors.

It was very kind, Clotilda thought, but not a collection of which she could be particularly proud, and she could only hope that they would not look too meagre if they were put on show at the wedding festivities.

But all these minor things paled into insignificance beside the moment when she had to say goodbye to Swallow.

Regardless of her aunt's protests, she rode her horse every day until she finally left the Castle.

To save argument, she rode at six o'clock in the morning until breakfast time.

When the dressmakers, the seamstresses, the maids, and the Ladies-in-Waiting were dropping with fatigue making alterations to her gowns, packing and doing all the thousand things that needed to be done before she could leave, Clotilda rode again.

Only at the last moment when she said goodbye to Swallow after riding him before breakfast did she break down.

"How can I leave you? Oh, darling, how can I leave you?" she sobbed.

As if Swallow understood how unhappy she was, he nuzzled against her, which made her cry more, and she wept until her eyes were swollen.

She managed to stop her tears as she said goodbye to her uncle and aunt, but as she drove away from the castle she looked back, almost expecting to see Swallow in the courtyard saying goodbye, and she wept again.

The Baroness, who was travelling in the same carriage, was tactful enough to sit in silence until Clotilda could control herself.

Then as they drove to London, she talked to her quietly of other things of the countries her father had travelled in and that she had known in her diplomatic days with her husband, and of the people who had lived in them.

Clotilda knew she was being kind and by the time they reached London she was determined to behave as was expected of her.

They arrived late in the evening and there was only just time to change for dinner, which the Minister and his wife had been tactful enough to confine to a quiet gathering of those who resided in the Ministry.

The next morning there was a short farewell ceremony before everybody departed for Tilbury to see Clotilda off.

The Marquis was not present and Clotilda did not give him a thought, although she heard the Countess say to her husband that she thought it was disgraceful that he insisted on making his own way to the ship rather than coming with them.

"Weybourne, my dear, is a law unto himself," the Minister replied.

They were speaking in their own language, but Clotilda understood.

She had found to her delight when she talked to the Baroness that it was not at all difficult for her.

The Bãlutik language was in fact a mixture of Albanian and Serbian with a lot of Romanian words and one or two Greek, all languages in which Clotilda was proficient.

She insisted upon talking with the Baroness every moment they were together, and she knew, although she still had some way to go, that an ordinary conversation in the language of her future country would present no difficulties.

"I suppose Prince Fredrick, even if he prefers to speak German, can speak Bãlutik?" she asked.

"I do not think so," the Baroness replied. "I think actually he feels it is somewhat beneath his dignity to speak any language but his own."

"How ridiculous!" Clotilda exclaimed before she could prevent herself.

Then, because she was sure the Baroness was shocked, she quickly changed the subject.

Now as they reached the outskirts of Tilbury and she knew it was only a question of time before she boarded the battleship that would take her away from England forever, Clotilda suddenly felt panic-stricken.

Why was she doing this? Why had she let herself be caught up in a net that was carrying her from her own world into another one?

She had no wish to be a reigning Princess, and while she had often thought of marriage, she had always imagined she would marry somebody who was a younger edition of her father.

She had wanted a man who had the same interests as herself, and who was very unconventional when it came to social consequence or protocol of any sort.

'I must have been crazy to agree!' she thought frantically.

Then she knew the truth was that whether she agreed or disagreed it would not have made any difference.

She had been forced into a position where she had to do as she was told.

'It is very German,' she told herself, 'to make people obey, and to make sure they do so, not allow them time to think!'

Because she wanted to scream and open the carriage door and jump out, she clasped her hands very tightly in her lap.

Her face was pale and her eyes frightened as she had her first glimpse of the warship which had been sent. It was, she thought, like a prison wagon to carry her to her destination.

Actually, it looked rather pretty.

It was, she learned, a modern ship, built only a few years ago, and while there were still two masts with sails, the Man-o'-War certainly looked very much a battleship.

Their carriage drew up beside the gangplank, and she noticed flags and bunting as she stepped from the carriage. A band played first the British, then the Bãlutik National Anthem, as everybody stood to attention.

Then the Minister introduced her to the Captain of the ship and his officers, who all greeted her in broken English with unmistakably guttural German accents.

She was then taken on a tour of the ship to admire the bridge, the guns and the lifeboats.

Finally she was taken down to the Saloon, where there was a presentation of a model of the Man-o'-War to her and Prince Fredrick as a wedding present from every man serving on the ship.

Clotilda made a short speech of thanks and, although she felt shy, she had had experience in the past of opening the Flower Show in the village and the Bazaar held every winter for the poor and needy.

She knew therefore how to make her voice carry, and when she had finished the Minister said to her.

"That was absolutely excellent! I had a feeling, Lady Clotilda, you would prove a very good speaker?"

"I wish that were true," Clotilda replied, "and it is something I hope I do not have to do very often."

Just as she was being offered a glass of champagne, she saw the Captain hurry out on deck and realised that somebody else had arrived.

A few seconds later the Captain returned to the Saloon with the newcomer who she knew without being told, was the Marquis of Weybourne.

He was not in the least what she had expected.

He seemed to tower over every other man in the party and was dressed with an elegance that was distinctive because he appeared to be unconscious of his appearance.

He seemed almost overwhelmingly authoritative and at the same time very distinguished.

Clotilda could not explain to herself what she felt, but he seemed to dwarf everybody else until they appeared to vanish, and it was impossible to take her eyes from him.

The Minister hurried to greet him saying,

"I was just becoming worried, Marquis, in case you had lost your way."

"I left London rather late," the Marquis said in a bored voice, "but my horses did their best to prevent you from sailing without me."

"That we could certainly not have done!" the Captain assured him as if he had spoken seriously.

As they spoke, they seemed to propel the Marquis across the Saloon towards Clotilda, who was standing at the far end of it beside a table on which rested the model of the Man-o'-War.

Now, as she waited, she could not help feeling that she was very glad there was to be one English person with her when she arrived in Bãlutik.

However impressive Prince Fredrick might be, the Marquis would undoubtedly uphold the British Crown very much to its advantage.

"Lady Clotilda," the Minister was saying, "may I present the Marquis of Weybourne who, as you know, is to accompany you to Bãlutik and represent Her Gracious Majesty and His Royal Highness the Prince Consort at your wedding."

Clotilda curtsied and put out her hand eagerly.

To her surprise however the Marquis who had bowed his head to her seemed almost reluctant to take her hand and for a moment it was suspended in front of him in mid-air.

Then as she felt his fingers hard and strong enfold hers, she knew from the expression in his eyes that the Marquis of Weybourne was looking at her with contempt, and what appeared also to be dislike.

For a moment she could not imagine such a thing was possible.

Then in a cold and distant voice he said,

"My good wishes, Lady Clotilda, and may I hope that you will be very happy with your chosen bridegroom?"

There was something again contemptuous, cynical, and almost sarcastic in the way he spoke, which gave Clotilda a shock.

'Why,' she asked herself, 'should he speak to me in such a manner?'

And why should she be so acutely aware of his feelings and know that, though he had never met her before, he disliked her.

She was certain she was right in her supposition, for the Marquis, without saying any more, turned to greet the Countess and other members of the staff who had come down from London. There were also present the Ambassador of Austria, the Ministers of Bulgaria and Serbia, and to Clotilda's delight, the Ambassador of Romania.

She was sure he must know of her great-grandmother's family and as soon as he was introduced she chatted away to him in his own language.

They talked of the beauty of the country and the horses which she and her father had enjoyed riding when she had visited Romania with him.

She had been fifteen at the time, but she felt as she talked to the Ambassador that it was only yesterday, and she told herself she would always feel at home in the country to which some of her blood belonged.

"When you are married you must persuade His Royal Highness to bring you to Romania," the Ambassador said.

"I am hoping to visit many, many places in the Balkans of which Papa talked so often, in addition to those I have already been in myself," Clotilda answered.

"It will certainly be a surprise to them that like your father, you can speak their language, and may I congratulate you, My Lady, on how fluent you are in mine!"

"That is what I am delighted to hear," Clotilda smiled. "I was afraid that since the death of my father and my mother I would have forgotten the languages which, when I was young, were as familiar to me as English."

"I only wish you could have reigned in my country," the Ambassador sighed, "instead of in one that becomes more German year by year."

When he had spoken, a look of consternation came over his face and Clotilda knew that because they were speaking in Romanian he had forgotten he should not criticise her future husband.

The Ambassador coughed to hide his embarrassment and said,

"You know if there is any way in which I can ever serve you, Lady Clotilda, I should be only too willing and honoured to do so."

Then as if he were ashamed at having betrayed his true feelings about Bãlutik, he moved away as somebody else came up to talk to Clotilda.

All too soon the Captain made it clear that the ship should get under way.

It took some time for the guests to say goodbye and as they went down the gangplank to where the carriages were waiting Clotilda longed to be going with them.

Instead, with the Baroness beside her, she stood and waved, while with the band playing, they moved very slowly towards the entrance of the dock.

It was only after she had waved until her arm ached and the crowd of people on the quay were out of sight that Clotilda realised the Marquis was nowhere to be seen.

As far as she could remember, he had taken no part in the ceremonies.

She suspected that instead he had either gone to the bridge to watch the Captain taking the ship out to sea, or else had retired to his own cabin.

The Baroness insisted that they go below.

"I am hoping, Lady Clotilda, we shall not have rough weather in the Channel at any rate," she was saying, "for I must confess that I am not a good sailor."

"Then I am sorry for you," Clotilda said, "because I love being at sea and it can never be too rough for me!"

The Baroness did not reply and Clotilda had the idea that she felt seasick at the mere thought of anybody enjoying the pitch and toss of a vessel.

Most people also found it intolerable when a ship rolled.

Below Clotilda found that she had been given the best cabin in the ship, which she was certain was the Captain's and which took up the whole of the stern.

In her bedroom was the traditional four-poster, despite the fact they were on a Man-o'-War.

There was a small cabin next door with a long table in the middle of it, at which she would eat, and several comfortable armchairs battened down to the deck.

Her maid, Greta, had already unpacked the trunk that contained her clothes for the voyage.

This was another person to whom Clotilda could speak Bãlutik, and she said to her now,

"Are you a good sailor, Greta?"

"I try to be, Gracious Lady," Greta replied.

"Then you and I will not be afraid of the Bay of Biscay," Clotilda laughed, "and I cannot believe this ship is not very seaworthy. What was it like on the voyage out?"

"A little rocky!" Greta replied, and they both laughed.

Because the Baroness had gone to her own cabin Clotilda talked with Greta, who she discovered was a very experienced lady's maid, and had been brought back from retirement to come to England for her.

"Do you mean to say you left your husband and family?" Clotilda exclaimed in astonishment.

Greta made an elegant gesture with her hands.

"I had no choice, Gracious Lady."

"What do you mean by that?"

"His Royal Highness said I was to come to look after you. He had known me when I was in attendance on one of the poor princess's Ladies-in-Waiting, who taught me to be very efficient."

The way Greta spoke, as if she were embarrassed by the question, made Clotilda think there was something strange about her position.

Also, it seemed extraordinary that she should have been forced to come back to work at the Prince's command.

"You must have impressed His Royal Highness very much," she said tentatively.

"His Royal Highness found me useful," Greta said in a hard voice.

Then as if she were eager to change the subject she asked,

"What will the Gracious Lady wear this evening for dinner?"

"I have so many gowns," Clotilda replied, "that I cannot remember most of them. You choose me a suitable one, Greta, and I hope that I will be admired in it?"

She thought as she spoke that perhaps she had mistaken the way the Marquis had looked at her and hoped that when she saw him again he would be more pleasant.

But later, when she went into the sitting room to find both him and the Captain waiting for her, she realised he was just as disdainful as he had been before.

It was not a large party, but there were the Baroness, the Marquis and an *aide-de-camp,* Major Bernstein, who had been sent to represent the Army, the Captain and his Second-in-Command.

Because the Captain spoke very little English and the Commander none, it was easier for everybody to converse in German than to struggle with broken English or Bãlutik, which Clotilda realised was known only to the Baroness.

The Marquis had quite a good command of German, and Clotilda, although she disliked the language because her father had always said it was ugly, could speak it fluently.

She thought the Marquis seemed surprised that she was not tongue-tied and could join in the conversation, which was however mostly about the ship they were on and the Fleet which was being built at Prince Fredrick's command.

"We will have another battleship and destroyers in the near future," the Captain announced, "but of course they are expensive, and being so far from the sea, the Bãlutikians dislike being taxed for ships they never see."

"I cannot really imagine why you want such a large Navy," Clotilda remarked.

There was a little pause, then the Captain replied,

"His Royal Highness is sure that sooner or later all the Balkan countries will have to fight against aggression."

"From whom?" Clotilda enquired.

She remembered her father saying it was Germany who was menacing the smaller states, and their Federation was trying to incorporate each one of them in turn so that they would be to all intents and purposes under the German flag.

There was a pregnant silence before the Captain with a rather nervous look at the Marquis replied,

"I am afraid, Lady Clotilda, I am very ignorant of politics, but I am sure His Royal Highness will be looking forward to telling you of his ideas and ambitions, about which he is very positive."

Clotilda thought the Captain had evaded answering an uncomfortable question very cleverly, and she knew as she saw a glint in the Marquis's eyes that he was laughing at her for being outwitted.

'I hate him!' she told herself. 'Why should he be so unkind to me?'

At the same time, she had to admire him, as she realised that once again he dwarfed everybody in the cabin.

She noticed too that when he did speak there was a respectful silence, almost as if he were Royalty.

However, she was still aware that he was angry, contemptuous and, of course, cynical.

Although she could hardly believe it was something she had done, she was aware from the note in the Marquis's voice when he spoke to her and the expression in his eyes exactly what he was feeling.

Somehow it made her depression and apprehension for the future worse than it was already.

As soon as possible she said goodnight and retired to her own cabin, where Greta was waiting for her.

"Did they admire you, Gracious Lady?" she asked eagerly.

"No, Greta," Clotilda replied "Nobody paid me a compliment! All they could think about was ships?"

Greta laughed.

"That is like men! They think only of their own interests and women are not important – except in bed?"

She had spoken without thinking, then as if she felt she had been impertinent, she said,

"Pardon, Gracious Lady. That is something I should not have said."

"No, Greta, you can say to me exactly what you like and what you think," Clotilda replied "I am very sad and lonely at the moment, and I want you to talk to me as if I were a friend. That will make me feel better."

She realised that the maid's warm heart was touched as she replied,

"I am sorry for you, Gracious Lady, very, very sorry for you. They should not have asked anybody so young or so beautiful to be the bride of His Royal Highness."

There was a little pause, then Clotilda said,

"Tell me the truth, Greta. Is the Prince popular in Bãlutik?"

Greta busied herself undoing Clotilda's gown at the back.

"Tell me," Clotilda insisted as Greta did not speak.

Again, there was a long pause before Greta said,

"Gracious Lady asks me to speak as a friend, and as a friend I must tell the truth."

"Please do," Clotilda begged.

"The Prince is very harsh, very strict, and this we do not understand. We are a happy people, we laugh, we cry, we sing, but the Prince is German, not like us!"

It was what she might have known, Clotilda thought.

When she was alone in the darkness and she could hear the engines churning away below her, she wanted to turn the ship round and go home.

What she had suspected was true, the Prince was not a popular ruler and she was merely being used as a pawn in order to improve his position in Bãlutik.

"Why should *I* have to do this?" she asked. "Why me?"

It was a question that men and women have asked all through the ages, and for which there has never seemed to be an answer.

As the ship sailed her on through the darkness of the night, Clotilda lay awake.

She knew she was afraid, even more than she had been before, of what awaited her when she reached Bãlutik.

CHAPTER FOUR

As soon as they were out of the Channel and into the Bay of Biscay the weather became progressively rougher.

First the Baroness no longer came into meals but just lay in her cabin suffering.

Then the Captain and the Commander were obliged to be constantly on the bridge, the *aide-de-camp* vanished and Clotilda found herself alone with the Marquis.

The first meal at which this happened was dinner, and despite the roughness of the sea she put on one of her pretty new gowns and went into the adjacent cabin to find that he was looking resplendent in his evening clothes.

"I am afraid the rest of the company has deserted us," he said.

Clotilda thought the way he spoke showed very clearly that he regretted it, and as she sat down at the table realising the stewards were ready to bring in their dinner she said,

"I am so sorry for people who feel seasick, and I imagine that is something that never happens to you."

"I would not say never," the Marquis replied, "but I have a yacht of my own and I have had some very rough and at times rather frightening voyages in it."

"How lucky you are!" Clotilda said. "Papa travelled to a great many parts of the world and when I was old enough I went with him, but we could never afford to travel in anything but the cheapest and usually the most uncomfortable way."

The Marquis looked at her in surprise as she added,

"I loved every moment of it, and it has been very dull since first Papa became a Duke and had no time to travel and then he died."

There was a throb in her voice, although she did not realise it, that was very moving.

After a moment the Marquis said,

"I had no idea you were so widely travelled, Lady Clotilda. I had expected to find this was the first time you had been at sea."

"Shall I say it is the first time I have ever travelled in such luxury!" Clotilda replied. "I find a Man-o'-War a very exciting form of transport!"

"I presume because there are so many men on board," the Marquis said in his most sarcastic tone.

Clotilda looked at him wide-eyed, then she replied,

"I was actually thinking that travelling in itself is exciting, but what I enjoyed most with Papa was meeting the ordinary people in the countries we visited, talking to them, and listening to their problems and their joys."

She spoke quite simply and was not aware that the Marquis looked at her in astonishment.

Then he said almost as if he wished to find fault,

"How do you mean – speaking to them? I have heard that your father spoke many languages well, but I can hardly believe that at your age you are very proficient!"

"What language would you like to talk to me in?" Clotilda replied in Turkish.

The Marquis did not answer and she went on in Greek.

"I thought your German was very good, but as a language it has something unpleasant about it and I am delighted we have not to speak it tonight."

Unexpectedly the Marquis laughed.

"You have made your point, Lady Clotilda," he said, "and I apologise for doubting your capabilities."

Then his eyes hardened as he said,

"I can quite see why you wish to reign over a Balkan country."

There was a little pause before Clotilda replied.

"I had no thought of doing any such thing!"

As she spoke she realised the stewards who were waiting on them came from Bãlutik, and she knew it would be a great mistake to say anything they might understand and perhaps repeat amongst themselves.

Instead, she said quickly,

"Do tell me which country you have enjoyed most on your visits abroad, and which you would wish to return to."

As if the Marquis understood she was being tactful, he answered her question and they had quite an animated discussion about the relative attractions of the East, of which Clotilda had very little knowledge, and of Africa, which she knew as well as he did.

"Do you really mean to say," he asked, "that you journeyed with your father over the desert? I can hardly believe it!"

"I would like to prove it to you," Clotilda said, "and I only wish we could order this ship to make a stop along the North African coast."

She gave a little sigh as she said,

"I sometimes feel homesick for the hot, dry air, the sands stretching out into infinity, and the feeling that there is no yesterday and no tomorrow."

As she spoke, she thought that was what she wanted at the moment, for if there were no tomorrow she would not have to go to Bãlutik and marry Prince Fredrick.

The Marquis was looking at her, thinking as he did so that her eyes were very revealing.

Then as he sat back comfortably in the chair that was battened down to the deck, holding a glass of brandy in his hand, he said,

"I am sure you are looking forward to the enthusiasm and acclaim of your new subjects."

Now the cynical note was back in his voice and Clotilda was aware that once again he was being unpleasant.

She rested her elbows on the table and cupping her chin in her hands looked not at the Marquis but across the cabin, seeing the portrait of Prince Fredrick.

She wished she could tell the Marquis how frightened she felt of what was happening to her and how she longed to talk about it to somebody like her father, who would understand.

Instead, as if she thought she should warn him, she said,

"All the stewards come from Bãlutik, and I believe the rest of the crew too with the exception of the officers, I am therefore being very careful what I say in front of them."

The Marquis raised his eyebrows.

"Are you reprimanding me, Lady Clotilda, for being indiscreet?"

"No, of course not," Clotilda said quickly. "At the same time, just as to your surprise I speak many languages, so I am well aware that anything we might say about Bãlutik will instantly be repeated throughout the ship and will of course be repeated again when we reach our destination."

She was thinking as she spoke of how her father had always told her that gossip not only in Eastern countries but in European also, was carried on the wind.

"A careless word can often cost lives," he had said to her once.

Clotilda had therefore always been very careful when they stayed in foreign houses in case even when they were talking privately to one another somebody was listening.

"Russian Palaces have hollow walls," her father had said, "and the same applies to Turkey, Persia, and of course Africa, where there is always somebody with big ears!"

They both laughed and Clotilda thought now that it would be a great mistake if the Marquis tempted her into being indiscreet.

At the same time, in a strange manner she could not understand, she wanted to talk to him confidentially and most of all to feel that he was sympathetic to her.

She was well aware that for a little while the sarcastic, cynical note had left his voice, but would return again when he spoke of the position she would occupy as the Prince's wife.

"I suppose you know," he said when they had been silent for a little while, "that it is really incorrect for you to be dining here alone with me. I cannot understand why His Royal Highness did not send a younger woman to chaperon you."

"I do not feel the need to be chaperoned," Clotilda said. "It is only extraordinary that the Prince should have dragged the Baroness out of retirement when she is so old and not in good health, and also forced Greta, my lady's maid, a married woman with four children, to leave them because he thought she had the right experience to tend to my needs."

"I should have thought that was very considerate," the Marquis remarked.

"As regards me, but not them," Clotilda said quickly.

"But of course as the bride you are all-important!"

Again, Clotilda thought he was being unpleasant about it.

"If it worries you being alone with me," she said, "I could of course eat in my cabin."

"It does not worry me," the Marquis said sharply. "But I have to think of your reputation."

Clotilda gave a little laugh.

"I believe, My Lord, you are actually thinking of yours. My uncle and aunt were very surprised when you were chosen to escort me!"

The Marquis frowned and she thought it was because he thought her impertinent for thinking such a thing.

Suddenly she felt it was impossible to spend the rest of the voyage being careful of everything she said.

Impulsively she turned her face to look at him.

"Please, My Lord," she said in a small voice, "c-could we not try to be friends for the short time we are on this ship? You are the only person aboard of the same nationality as myself and before I enter a strange country where I have never been before and from which I shall never be free again, I want to have some happy memories."

She knew as she finished speaking that the Marquis was looking at her in astonishment. Then he said in a different voice from his usual dry tone,

"I must apologise, Lady Clotilda, if I have upset you in any way or made you think I have not been – friendly."

There was a little pause before the last word and Clotilda said,

"Forgive me but I know you did not wish to come on this voyage in the first place, and also that you disapprove of my marrying Prince Fredrick."

The Marquis stiffened, then he stared at her.

"I am not admitting you are right," he said, "only asking why you think those things."

Clotilda smiled and made a gesture with her hand.

"I suppose I am using my instinct and perhaps being perceptive I do not wish you to admit anything, but that is what I am sure you are feeling and there is nothing I can do about it."

"I can only apologise again," the Marquis said, "if I have given you the wrong impression."

"Was it really wrong?" Clotilda enquired.

Now she looked directly into his eyes and she knew he would not look away.

For a moment neither of them spoke, then he said,

"I would like to reply that I will do anything in my power to make you as happy as possible until you reach Bãlutik."

Because it was getting late she thought it was only right that she should retire.

She left the Saloon and when she was in bed next door she was aware that the Marquis remained for a long time alone before he too finally went to bed.

'He is very strange,' she thought to herself, 'and yet in a way it is comforting to have him here, if only because I am frightened of the future, and of Prince Fredrick.'

The bad weather continued until they reached Gibraltar. Here the Captain informed the Marquis they were stopping in harbour because there were various things that had been smashed during the storms, which had to be replaced.

Clotilda was delighted.

"It is a long time since I have been to Gibraltar," she said, "but I remember the shops and how attractive they were."

She did not add that neither she nor her father had any money at the time to spend.

But there had been nothing to stop them looking, and she had enjoyed seeing the beautifully embroidered shawls that came from Hong Kong and China, even though she could not afford to buy one of them.

The Marquis was standing against the rails, looking up at the high rock towering above them and the English soldiers and sailors moving about in the harbour, when a small voice beside him said.

"Please My Lord could you possibly take me ashore for a little while?"

"The Baroness is indisposed?" he asked.

"She is not at all well," Clotilda replied, "and as Greta is looking after her, there is nobody I can ask except you."

"Then of course I am only too willing to oblige."

Clotilda flashed him a radiant smile and ran down to her cabin.

When she came back, she was wearing a very pretty bonnet to match her thin gown and carrying a small handbag.

She walked down the gangplank to find that the Marquis had ordered an open carriage drawn by one horse to take them from the harbour to the shops.

"This is very extravagant," she said. "We could easily have walked."

"People of importance do not walk about in the crowd!" the Marquis replied.

"But I am not important yet."

"You are to those you have left behind on the ship," the Marquis remarked.

She was silent. Then she said,

"If you think I am too important to go shopping, you are mistaken. I want to buy a present for the Baroness and also one for Greta."

"And what about yourself?" the Marquis enquired.

"What more could I possibly require?" Clotilda replied. "But I know what it is to be poor and unable to afford to spend even a few corns on luxuries, and that is what I want to give the two people who have been looking after me."

The Marquis helped her choose a very pretty, embroidered bag for the Baroness and a blouse, also embroidered, for Greta.

"Papa said the next time we came here, if he was with me, he would give me one of those beautiful shawls," Clotilda said almost as if she were speaking to herself.

She was looking at a display of them in one of the shops along the water's edge, and the Marquis said sharply, as if he thought she were pretending,

"Surely now you can afford anything you want?"

"Only if I spend His Royal Highness's money," Clotilda answered, "and that I have no intention of doing."

Almost as if the Marquis had questioned her, although he had said nothing, she added,

"What I have bought for the Baroness and Greta is with my own money, but I have comparatively little with me, and I feel it will have to last a very long time!"

Without his saying anything, she was aware that the Marquis was thinking she was putting on an act.

She knew he was looking at the very expensive gown she was wearing and her bonnet in the very latest style that went with it.

"I do not suppose anybody has told you, My Lord," she said, "but contrary to every tradition of propriety, His Royal Highness empowered his Minister in London to purchase my trousseau for me."

She saw the astonishment in his eyes and added,

"Because there was only a week in which to do everything, I could hardly refuse, and anyway my uncle could not have afforded even a twentieth of what I now possess."

"You surprise me, Lady Clotilda!" the Marquis said at length.

"I too am surprised," Clotilda said, "and, if I am truthful, humiliated, but there was nothing I could do about it – nothing!"

They returned to the carriage and as they drove back the Marquis, as if he had been thinking over what she had said, asked,

"Why did you not refuse to marry the Prince? Or was the allurement of a crown, even a small one, so enticing that nothing else was of any consequence?"

For the first time since they had been speaking together that morning the sarcasm was back in his voice and Clotilda said sharply,

"Can you really be so stupid as to think that I had a choice? The Queen had given her consent, although somewhat belatedly, the Minister informed us, having thought it over for a long time, and as His Royal Highness is determined to be married the moment I arrive in Bãlutik, there was no time to think or prevaricate. Besides, you must be aware that nobody would have listened to me."

"Is that the truth?"

The Marquis asked the question in a way which Clotilda felt was as if he were searching deeply not into her words, but into her mind.

"Of course it is the truth!" she said "But I did not know…"

She stopped and said quickly,

"Even though you have promised to be my friend, I know I must not say anything indiscreet, but there has been nobody I could talk to and my uncle and aunt, the Duke and Duchess, were of course absolutely delighted at the honour to the family."

She did not look at the Marquis as she spoke and at that moment the carriage drew up at the quay and they had to walk the short distance to the ship.

The Baroness came to luncheon that day and so there was no chance of a further intimate conversation with the Marquis.

Now that they were in smooth waters, the Captain and the *aide-de-camp* dined with them, and the conversation once again turned to ships in general and reminiscences about battles that had taken place in the Mediterranean.

When she went to bed, Clotilda wondered what the Marquis really thought about her, and if he had meant it when he said he would be friendly and make her happy.

'I expect it was just a diplomatic figure of speech,' she said with a little sigh.

Yet at the same time she hoped there would be another opportunity of being alone with him.

*

The next morning the Marquis awoke to the sound of drums.

He at first thought he was imagining the noise above the engines.

Then he realised they were in fact coming from the fore end of the ship and when he was dressed, instead of going to breakfast in the usual Saloon, he went to see what was happening.

As he had anticipated, he saw that one of the sailors was about to receive the standard punishment for some misdeed and was being tied to the mast of the ship, awaiting a flogging with the cat o'nine tails."

The Marquis was aware that the usual offences that resulted in flogging were theft, drunkenness and insolence, sleeping on watch and disobedience.

Although he had been often enough on ships while seamen had been flogged, he had always himself thought it an uncivilised method of maintaining discipline and disliked it intensely.

Now as the drumbeats seemed to accelerate, the man tied spread-eagled was waiting bare backed for the first stroke of the whip.

He was a tough, burly-looking seaman who had obviously been flogged before, for he bore the scars that the Marquis knew were referred to as a 'shell back'.

The cat o' nine tails descended, the drums rose to a crescendo, drowning any screams the victim might make, and as the blood spurted the Marquis turned away.

It was something he had no wish to look at, and as he did so he realised that he was not alone at his vantage point on the upper deck.

Without his having realised it, there was somebody else there.

He knew it was Clotilda and as he saw her running ahead of him wildly through the door that led down to their cabins, he followed, aware as he did so, that it was something she should not have seen.

No Captain with any sensitivity would have flogged a man aboard a ship where there were a number of women, especially somebody of Clotilda's importance.

As he reached the passage that led to their sleeping cabins, the Marquis thought Clotilda would have gone to her own.

Then as he reached it, he saw the door was open and that inside Greta with the help of Havers was making the four-poster bed.

He therefore walked into the next cabin and for a moment he thought it was empty.

Then he saw lying on the sofa, which was battened down at the far end under one of the portholes, there was a slight figure.

The Marquis shut the door behind him and as he walked towards Clotilda he saw she had her face hidden in a cushion.

Her hands were over both her ears, and he knew it was to keep out the noise of the drums and the screams of the man being flogged.

As he reached her, he realised she was trembling and he sat down on the end of the sofa and said very quietly,

"I am sorry, Lady Clotilda, that you should have witnessed what was certainly not a sight meant for your eyes."

"H-how could they do anything s-so bestial and cruel?" she asked.

"It is the usual punishment on any naval vessel, even our own," the Marquis replied. "I am glad to say however there is a great deal of opposition to it, and it has already been suggested in Parliament that it should be abandoned."

"It is wicked?"

The Marquis listened, then he said,

"It is all over now I can no longer hear the drums, and I think it was only twelve lashes, which is a light sentence."

"How can anything with that terrible whip be light?" Clotilda asked in a whisper.

Now she took her hands away from her ears and turned round.

The Marquis could see she was very pale, and there was a stricken look in her eyes.

She was not crying, but he was aware she was still trembling, and he knew the whole episode had been a shock to which she should not have been subjected.

"I will speak to the Captain," he said, "and I will see that this does not take place again, at least not while you are aboard."

There was a silence for a moment. Then Clotilda said in a voice he could hardly hear,

"Th-they said that was what the P-Prince l-liked?"

"Who said that?" the Marquis asked sharply.

"I-I heard two of the stewards talking," Clotilda explained, "b-but I did not know what it was about and that was why I went on d-deck to look."

The Marquis drew in his breath, wondering what she had heard.

After what Lord Toddington had told him, he was sure the Prince's erotic tastes were indulged not only in other countries, and it would be known in Bălutik what he was like.

Yet he could hardly believe that Clotilda as his wife would learn of her husband's unpleasant habits, and he was sure that the Prince would not beat his own wife.

Then he asked himself if he really was sure, and as he looked at Clotilda's pale face, shocked eyes, and hands that were still trembling, he had an almost irresistible impulse to turn the ship around and order the Captain to take them back to England.

Then he knew to do such a thing was not only impossible, but would cause a diplomatic furore, which would be so scandalous that he would be ostracised from Society, if not exiled for life.

As he rose to his feet the Marquis went to a porthole to look out at the blue waters of the Mediterranean, the sun golden on the distant coastline.

'What can I do?' he asked himself. *'What the Devil can I do?'*

Then behind him he heard Clotilda say,

"I-I suppose you are thinking that I am behaving very badly and I know people who are Royal do not show their emotions whatever happens but I-I cannot b-bear cruelty!"

"Nor can I," the Marquis replied.

Now Clotilda was no longer lying on the sofa, but sitting on one end of it, and he crossed the cabin to sit down near her.

"Now, listen to me, Lady Clotilda," he said. "I know this has been a great shock and something, as I said, you should not have seen, but I hope you will try to forget it. At the same time, you will find in your new life that the Germans are very strict disciplinarians."

"They may be strict," Clotilda replied, "but they should not enjoy a man's suffering however much he may deserve it."

The Marquis knew she was thinking of what she had overheard the stewards saying.

He thought it was very unfortunate that they should not have realised their future Princess understood their language, and he would make certain at once that everybody aboard was aware of her linguistic abilities.

"I am sure it is true to say," he said aloud, "that the Prince wants perfection around him, and does not like a man to avoid punishment for any real misdeed."

The Marquis knew as he spoke that Clotilda was not convinced, and he wondered what else the stewards had said that she had not related to him.

Sharply, because he was perturbed, he said,

"Forget it! This sort of thing should not concern you, and when you are reigning over Bălutik I am sure that your job will be to see that the hospitals are well run, that every child has the advantage of education and that if there are women's grievances, and I am sure there will be many, they can come to you for help."

"And do you think the Prince will let me help?" Clotilda asked. "As he is so old I doubt if he will listen to anything I have to say."

As this was what the Marquis suspected himself, he said almost angrily,

"It is no use anticipating things that may never happen. Any man who has a wife as beautiful as you will, if she is clever, listen to her and wish to please her."

As if he could bear the conversation no longer, he walked from the cabin, leaving Clotilda alone.

For a moment she just stared at the closed door and wondered why he had left her so abruptly.

Then she repeated to herself beneath her breath,

"As beautiful as you!"

So he did admire her after all! And somehow, although it seemed extraordinary, she was no longer trembling and the sunshine seemed to fill the cabin.

*

There were no further uncomfortable incidents as they sailed on until they reached Naples.

Then the Captain said to the Marquis,

"I must apologise, My Lord, for having to diverge so far from our direct course, but the damage that had to be repaired at Gibraltar is rather worse than I anticipated, and therefore we have to put into Naples to have some more repairs done before we proceed with all speed to where Her Ladyship's escort will be waiting for us."

"I think the answer is," the Marquis said with a smile, "that we will just have to wait. I am sure, Captain, your ship is more important than anything else."

"I thought you would understand, My Lord."

The Captain gave a sigh as he added,

"I doubt if His Royal Highness will?"

"It sounds as if he is a very hard taskmaster?"

"He expects everything to run exactly according to his wishes, My Lord," the Captain answered dryly, "and he does not consider an Act of God, or in this case the buffeting of the sea, an adequate excuse for not keeping to a schedule."

The Marquis laughed.

He found himself wondering how Clotilda would cope with German preciseness and punctuality for the rest of her life.

It was of course inevitable that she should have told him by this time about Swallow.

Because the Marquis had so many horses of his own that meant a great deal to him, he understood that for Clotilda the real misery of leaving England had been that she must leave Swallow behind.

"I know the grooms at the Castle will look after him as they always have," she said, "but he will not understand why I do not come back to him and I think horses are like us – if they love somebody they never forget them."

"I am sure that is true," the Marquis agreed.

"Swallow loves me as I love him," Clotilda said, "as I am sure I shall never, never love anybody else!"

The Marquis knew she was speaking from her heart, and he thought that with her beauty there was no doubt that a great number of men would in the years to come to fall in love with her.

'And of course,' he told himself, 'she with them?'

Then, as he thought about it, he knew she was not like other women he had known, who accepted lover after lover until it became their chief amusement in life.

He had always considered it an amusing and pleasant way of passing the time, which sometimes ended in tears, but more often than not was a delightful episode to remember.

Then he found himself asking if that was the real love, which had been written about by the poets, depicted by artists, and made immortal by musicians.

It was a love he had never known, but which he had once believed in many years ago when he was young and idealistic and thought the woman he loved was the other half of himself and loved him as he loved her.

That he had been bitterly disillusioned was something he had never forgotten.

Now he could not help thinking that perhaps Clotilda was rather like he had been at the same age – reaching out towards a distant horizon and believing that by some miracle her dreams would come true.

'Like every other woman she will have to put up with second best,' he told himself cynically.

Yet as he watched Clotilda moving about the deck in the sunshine with a smile and a word for every seaman she encountered, he knew that for her to be awakened to the realities of love by a man like Prince Fredrick would be an even worse shock than what she had felt when she saw the seaman being flogged.

'There is nothing I can do, so I will not think about it,' the Marquis told himself.

But for the first time in his life he found it impossible to control his thoughts and, because they perturbed him, he spent as little time as possible in Clotilda's company.

He thought in consequence that two days before they reached Naples she looked at him reproachfully when they met in the Saloon.

There was no chance of talking intimately to her with everybody there and, as soon as the meal was over, he made some excuse to go up on the deck.

Naples was looking very beautiful despite the obvious poverty of many of its inhabitants.

It rose above a natural harbour and as they came into port the Marquis found Clotilda at his side, and she said to him with a little lift in her voice,

"The last time I was here Papa made me aware of the luminosity, which is different from anywhere else – in the world. He told me how the Greeks recognised it long before the Romans came."

"I see you are well read, Lady Clotilda," the Marquis replied.

"I wish that were true, for there is still so much more I want to know, so much more I have to learn."

"I think we all feel that when very wisely we educate ourselves," the Marquis said.

"Is that what you do?"

"Of course," he answered, "I am well aware that there are many subjects of which I am lamentably ignorant or, shall I say, have just enough knowledge to realise that I must learn a great deal more."

She laughed and she looked so lovely as she did so that the Marquis thought the man who taught her about love would have an intriguing and fascinating task.

Then he remembered that the Prince was German and that the Germans had none of the sensitivity or art of the French. In fact, the majority of them thought a woman's only function was to pander to their desires and was not expected to have any character or personality of her own.

'I am generalising, which is always wrong,' the Marquis told himself, 'and I am sure the Prince at his age is intelligent enough to know that he must approach anybody as young as Lady Clotilda gently and think more of her than of himself.'

Yet what Lord Toddington had said was inescapably in his mind, and quickly, as if to change the subject, he pointed out Vesuvius to Clotilda.

They talked of the lava that had rolled down the mountain covering Herculaneum and Pompeii, and the exciting excavations that had recently been started there.

As the Baroness had no wish to leave the ship for the rather sordid port that existed round the Quay, Clotilda made no effort to go ashore.

She sat on deck under an awning looking at the beauty of the view.

The Marquis 'stretched his legs' as he called it but did not go far and returned to the ship to be informed by the Captain that they would be able to sail at dawn, and there should be no further difficulties on their voyage to Bãlutik.

He was, however, too busy to join them at dinner, and the Baroness kept Clotilda and the Marquis amused with the tales of her husband's adventures as Ambassador to different countries and how happy they had been in France.

"I found Paris so gay and so civilised," she said wistfully, "and we in Bãlutik have a great affinity with the

French. Not that we are as cultured as they are, but we have the same instinct for beauty, and of course for love!"

She smiled a little reminiscently to herself as if she were thinking how much love had meant in her life.

The Marquis, glancing across the table at Clotilda, was aware of a frightened expression in her eyes.

Something had upset her, he could see, but not understanding what it was, he decided regretfully that it would be indiscreet to ask.

The Baroness retired, and when Clotilda too went to her cabin, he was alone.

He read the newspapers, which had come aboard at Naples, then, feeling it was hot inside his cabin, went out on deck.

It was dark, but every house in Naples had a light in it and he thought how lovely it looked with the stars glittering above and a crescent moon climbing up the sky.

Then looking down from the top deck he was aware that by the lower gangway a slight figure was leaving the ship.

He thought with a twist of his lips that one of the seamen must have had a woman on board, which was strictly against the German rule, though nevertheless such things happened.

The woman had a shawl over her head, and as he watched her walking away quickly a strange idea came to him, which he told himself was ridiculous.

And yet he thought that having seen Clotilda for so many days, he would have known the graceful movement of her body, which was different from that of any woman he knew.

On an impulse he walked to the top gangway which was used only by the Captain and the distinguished guests aboard the battleship.

There were seamen on duty who saluted him when he appeared and the Marquis said,

"I am going ashore for a short walk. Lend me your revolver?"

The man looked at him in surprise but was not disposed to argue with anyone so distinguished, especially the Marquis, who spoke in the authoritative tone of one who expected to be obeyed.

The seaman took his revolver from the holster where it hung at his hip and the Marquis slipped it into the pocket of his coat.

He hurried down the gangway and set off in pursuit of the woman with the shawl over her head.

She was almost out of sight and the quay where they were tied up was not very profusely lit, but with his long strides it was only a few moments before the Marquis could see her more clearly.

Now he was quite certain, although he had not seen her face, that it was Clotilda, but where she was going at this hour of the night, he had no idea.

He could hardly believe she had an assignation with a man, and yet why else should she go ashore at Naples of all places, and alone?

He saw her stop ahead of him to speak to an elderly woman.

She obviously asked a question and the woman being Neapolitan replied very volubly, finally pointing in the direction of a road a little way ahead.

Clotilda walked on and the Marquis followed, until at last when he had begun to think he must be mistaken, she stopped and went in through a lighted door, and he saw she had entered a pharmacy.

Through the glass window he could see her talking to an elderly man behind a narrow counter.

The shop was very small and in the window there were huge glass bottles filled, the Marquis was sure, with coloured water.

Behind the counter he could see innumerable little drawers all labelled on the outside with the name of their contents.

Watching, he was aware that Clotilda had asked for something that was causing a lot of trouble.

The pharmacist was obliged to get a ladder to climb up to the very top drawers, which were against the ceiling, to find what he required.

Finally, he handed over what had been asked for and the Marquis saw Clotilda paying him with money she had in a small purse.

He stepped aside into the shadows of the doorway so that she would not see him when she came out.

She opened the door and he heard her voice as she said,

"Goodnight and thank you, *Signore,* I am very grateful to you."

She spoke in Italian and the Pharmacist replied,

"You will be very careful, *Signorina,* and not take more than I have told you is safe."

"Yes, I will remember, *Signore,* and thank you again."

She stepped out into the roadway, shutting the door behind her, then began to walk downhill towards the quay.

She had not gone far when a man came from the side of the road towards her.

He stopped in front of her and the Marquis stopped too, not wishing to interfere unless it was necessary.

A moment later he saw Clotilda try to run away from the man, but he reached out and caught hold of her arm.

She gave a scream, and the Marquis heard her say,

"Let me go! You have no right to stop me!"

By this time the man had hold of her and having dragged her across the road was taking her, the Marquis saw, towards an open space where there were no houses, but only darkness.

Clotilda was struggling, at the same time giving little screams of fear, but the man was large, and she was completely helpless in his hands.

"Leave that woman alone!" the Marquis said firmly, speaking Italian.

His voice came as a surprise both to Clotilda and to her attacker.

For a moment they were both still.

Then as the man, a rough individual, saw the revolver in the Marquis's hand, he turned and ran.

As he did so Clotilda flung herself at the Marquis and he knew she was trembling as she had when she had seen the man being flogged.

He put his arm around her and, as he saw her assailant disappearing into the darkness, he returned the revolver to his pocket.

By this time Clotilda's face was against his shoulder, the shawl over her head had fallen away in the struggle, and the starlight was on her fair hair.

"How could you have done anything so crazy, so mad, as to come here alone?"

The Marquis spoke sharply as if to a child, and Clotilda replied,

"I-I wanted to buy something."

"We will go back to the ship."

As he spoke, she took her head from his shoulder and with what he knew was a tremendous effort she turned in the direction of the sea.

With the Marquis's arm still around her they started to walk slowly down the road, keeping to the centre of it to avoid the shadows.

"What did you go to buy?" he asked at last.

There was silence and after a moment Clotilda answered.

"I-I cannot tell you."

"Why not?"

"Y-you will be angry with me."

"Would it matter if I were?"

"You-you will think I am a coward."

"I do not think you a coward, considering you were brave enough to walk about Naples alone at night," he said, "but I do think you very foolish and it is something you must promise me you will never do again."

"We are leaving in the morning."

"That is no answer, as you know," he replied. "I have no wish to bully you, Clotilda, but I want you to tell me what you bought."

He spoke very gently, and they were neither of them aware that he had used her Christian name without the prefix of her rank.

They walked on for quite a little way before Clotilda said in a voice he could hardly hear,

"I only bought something to take if I could not bear it any longer!"

"What do you mean?" the Marquis asked.

"M-my marriage?"

They reached the end of the quay and now the ship was in sight when the Marquis stopped.

He put both his hands on Clotilda's shoulders and turned her round to face him.

The moonlight was on her face, and he thought as she looked up at him nervously that she was very beautiful, and yet somehow insubstantial, as if she were not real and might disappear at any moment.

Then he forced himself to say,

"Are you telling me that you bought poison?"

He knew the answer without Clotilda confirming it.

"But why?" he asked after a long pause. "Why now? What has suddenly upset you?"

She did not answer and after a moment he repeated,

"Tell me what has upset you?"

"It is something that Aunt Augusta said to me and also Greta."

She stopped.

"What did they tell you? I want you to tell me."

Clotilda made a little movement as if she would run away from him, but his hands were on her shoulders, and it was impossible for her to do so.

"Tell me!" the Marquis repeated. "As a friend, and if I am to help you, I must know."

"You will think it very stupid," Clotilda said after a moment, "b-but I do not know because Mama died when I was young what a man and a woman do when they make love but Aunt Augusta said I had to remember that my husband was my master and although he would do a lot of unpleasant things to me there was nothing I could do about it."

Her voice as she spoke was tremulous and the words seemed to come with little gasps.

"And what did your maid say?" the Marquis asked.

"She did not actually tell me, but I guessed," Clotilda said in a whisper, "that the reason why she said she had been 'useful' to the Prince was that he was having a love affair with her mistress who was Lady-in-Waiting to his w-wife?"

She made a sound like that of a small animal caught in a trap.

"I never thought… I never imagined that he might do that sort of thing when we were m-married," Clotilda said, "and if I disappoint him or if he does not like me, he might beat me as the stewards said that was what he enjoys doing himself!"

This, the Marquis knew, was a different story from the one she had told him before, and he knew it was because she felt embarrassed that she had only told him half the truth.

He wondered desperately what he could say, then Clotilda said piteously,

"I know you will despise me, I know you think I am a c-coward, which I am, but I only bought the poison so that if everything was really intolerable I-I could die and be with P-Papa!"

As she spoke the Marquis realised that she was almost collapsing with the intensity of her feelings, and because too she was frightened.

"We will talk about it tomorrow," he said. "I think now we should go back to the ship. No one, you understand, Clotilda, no one must know, not even the Baroness or your maid that you went ashore alone."

"I-I did not think anybody would see me."

"There are always sailors guarding the ship at night, and as they came from Bãlutik, nobody knows better than you do how much they will talk."

"Yes, of course I did not think."

They walked on and now as they neared the gangplank by which the Marquis had left the ship he said,

"I will take your arm in mine, and we will talk happily as if we have just been enjoying ourselves walking on shore in the night air and doing nothing more sinister."

He knew Clotilda trembled at the word.

Then, as he led her up the gangplank, he thought how small and helpless she was and that he too felt helpless.

'I have to do something,' he told himself, 'but God knows what?'

CHAPTER FIVE

Following the repairs to the ship in Naples, the Man-o'-War seemed to move with more speed than it had before, and as the sea was calm the Marquis was aware that the Captain was delighted with their progress.

"I shall not get into as much trouble as I anticipated, My Lord!" he said in a tone of satisfaction.

The Marquis however had found it difficult to sleep not only the night of his being ashore with Clotilda, but the following one.

He found himself wishing that a miracle would prevent them from arriving in Bãlutik.

He had learned from Major Bernstein exactly what had been planned.

"As we unfortunately have to pass through Albanian territory, My Lord," the Major said, "there will be very little fuss when the ship docks. In fact, I doubt if any Albanian dignitaries will be on the quay."

"What trouble is His Highness having with Albania?" the Marquis asked.

The Major shrugged his shoulders.

"They are a tiresome country, and so for that matter are Montenegro and Serbia when it comes to discussion on defence."

The Marquis was sure that Prince Fredrick wanted to put his country more or less on a war footing, while the other Balkan States wished only to live in peace and prosperity, and not trouble themselves with anything so upsetting as war."

He tactfully said nothing, and the Major went on.

"There will be just a small detachment of soldiers waiting for us, with nobody of importance from Bãlutik until we have completed half the journey, which will bring us to the Castle, where we are to stay the night."

The Marquis looked surprised.

"I should have thought," he said after a moment, "that at least your Foreign Secretary would be in attendance on Lady Clotilda?"

"You must understand, My Lord," the Major said in a dictatorial tone that the Marquis found irritating, "His Royal Highness has encountered a lot of hostility from the Albanian and the Montenegro governments. He therefore has no wish to ask any favours of them."

"No, of course not," the Marquis agreed soothingly, realising this was a sore point. "Go on with what has been planned."

"We must therefore proceed as quickly as possible through the pass in the mountains that will take us to the Castle, which is approximately ten miles from Bãlutik."

The Major's voice became more impressive as he said,

"There Her Ladyship will be met by the Prime Minister, the Foreign Secretary and the Generals commanding our Army."

"And Prince Fredrick?" the Marquis enquired.

"His Royal Highness will greet his future bride the moment she sets foot on Bãlutik soil," the Major replied.

"Then they will proceed together in a procession towards the Palace, with the route lined with troops and populace."

The Marquis repressed a desire to ask whether the populace would cheer spontaneously or whether it would be under order, but merely accepted the plan without comment.

He was however extremely perturbed about Clotilda.

Ever since he had seen her buy the poison in Naples, he had had little chance of talking to her alone because either the Baroness or Greta always seemed to be with her.

He realised too that Major Bernstein was preparing her for what she had to expect when she arrived in Bãlutik and was making her more frightened than she was already.

Because she had looked so pale and harassed after they returned to the ship following her expedition in the night, the Marquis had said very little.

In fact, although they had gone into the Saloon for a few seconds and he had given her something to drink, he had then said to her,

"Go to bed, Clotilda! There is nothing more exhausting than being emotionally as well as physically afraid, and I am sure that what you are anticipating is far worse than the reality."

He knew as he spoke that he was lying to comfort her, but there was nothing else he could do, and he felt, as she gave him a worried little smile, that she was making a great effort at self-control.

"Thank you for being so kind," she murmured.

Still holding the bottle of poison tightly in one hand, she went into her own cabin and shut the door behind her.

*

The next day, when the Marquis saw the dark lines under Clotilda's eyes, he knew that her emotions had taken their toll, and it would be best not to make things worse by talking about it.

Instead, he set himself out at mealtimes to be amusing and to talk interestingly about subjects which he knew she enjoyed and was glad when she responded.

At the same time, he was well-aware, as he was sure she was, that the hours were passing and that soon they would leave the ship. Then the prison walls would begin to close around her.

He tried to tell himself it was none of his business, and yet now in the darkness of his own cabin, with the sound of the engines moving them inexorably onwards, he had the feeling that the sands were running out and there was no longer any chance of saving her.

'Only a miracle, or God, could do that,' he told himself, and was surprised at how angry it made him feel.

The Albanian coastline, when they reached it, was extremely impressive with its high cliffs and the tops of the mountains towering above them.

Drina was quite a small port, as the Marquis guessed. But there were a few fishermen's cottages around it – and a few unimpressive, rather ugly municipal buildings.

As the Major had anticipated, there were no Albanian dignitaries to greet them, but the Bãlutik soldiers in their colourful uniforms looked smart, though somewhat theatrical.

There was an enormous amount of clicking of heels, clinking of rifles and saluting as Clotilda, followed by the Marquis, came down the gangplank.

Major Bernstein presented the Officer-in-Charge, then the Bãlutik National Anthem was played slowly and rather lugubriously by a small band.

When Clotilda had inspected the soldiers, with the Marquis walking a few paces behind her, the carriages were ready for them.

She found to her surprise that she was to travel with the Marquis in the first one, with Major Bernstein and the Officer-in-Charge of the troops sitting opposite them.

"What about the Baroness?" she asked.

The Marquis looked back to where the Baroness was being helped down the gangplank with what appeared to be some difficulty.

"She will follow in the next carriage," he replied.

"She is not at all well," Clotilda confided. "In fact, I suggested to her that she stay aboard the ship, but she would not agree."

"She will be all right," the Marquis said confidently, "and I understand it is not a long journey to the Castle."

"That is what the Major told me," Clotilda replied, "but it is all uphill, and Greta says the road is very bad."

There was nothing they could do about it, and the Marquis looked to see that the Baroness was helped into her carriage, which was identical to the one in which they were travelling.

Behind was a larger carriage that carried all the luggage as well as Havers and Greta.

The Marquis had expected that their escort would march the uphill miles to the Castle, but instead he saw they were provided with two brakes and thought this was actually a good sign of German efficiency.

Finally, the procession got under way with the first carriage in front carrying Clotilda, with the Baroness and the luggage, then the brakes with the soldiers.

Behind that there was a rough, open cart in which to the Marquis's amusement and, he thought, the disgust of the Major, there were a number of young girls and boys from Drina.

They had been standing watching Clotilda's arrival, and it was obvious they were curious and excited by the presence of the soldiers.

Now they were eager to follow to see what was happening, and when after travelling a little way, the Major ascertained they were still there, he said irritably,

"I hope they will soon grow bored with following us, I had no idea they would do anything so outrageous."

"I expect it is a new amusement for them," the Marquis said good-humouredly.

The Officer sitting with them in the carriage said,

"On His Royal Highness's instructions, we have made every effort to see that nobody locally and none of the troops were aware it was his bride who was arriving."

"Why?" the Marquis asked abruptly.

"His Royal Highness thought it incorrect for Her Ladyship to be acclaimed by another country before she had reached ours."

The Marquis thought privately that it was much more likely that the Prince thought the Albanians, who were a very fiery people, might be offensive to Clotilda in view of who she was marrying.

But he said aloud,

"I always found when I was in the Army that a military uniform is an irresistible attraction to young women whenever they see it, and I expect your soldiers are receiving all the attention and therefore Lady Clotilda will pass unnoticed."

"That is certainly what I hope," Major Bernstein replied. "His Royal Highness would be extremely annoyed if he knew what was happening."

"I imagine there would be no reason for anybody to tell him," the Marquis remarked, "so do not worry your head about it."

The Major looked down his nose as if he thought that was a typically English way of viewing what was a definite breach of orders and of etiquette.

They drove on in silence and the Marquis was aware that Clotilda was looking out through the window of the carriage wistfully.

He was sure she was thinking how delightful it would be if she could ride on Swallow instead of being cooped up in a vehicle in which there was little air and less sunshine.

He did not know this, but he was certain that was what she felt and as they passed some horses grazing by the roadside, she turned to look at him with a little smile and he knew he had been right.

Greta had also been right when she had said the road would be rough, and as soon as they were away from the harbour and had started to climb, the Marquis knew it was going to be a slow, painstaking journey.

The roadway had obviously suffered from the floods that had poured down it during the rainy season as well as from the snow when it melted after the winter was past.

The wheels of the carriage continually had to pass over huge stones, resulting in either Clotilda being thrown against him, or the Marquis against her. She was sure that by the end of the day there would be bruises on her arms.

She was looking exceedingly lovely, as Greta had told her, in a light travelling gown with a cloak over it of the same material.

Her very full skirts seemed to take up a great deal of room in the carriage, but there was still space for the Marquis's long legs.

Even though he was wearing the ordinary clothes of an English gentleman, Clotilda thought he looked far more impressive than the two Germans, despite the fact they wore such elaborate uniforms, resplendent with so many medals.

They drove on and after a time, as there seemed to be no point in talking, everybody lapsed into silence.

Finally, when they had reached what seemed for the moment to be almost the top of the road, the horses were brought to a standstill.

The Major and the other officer got out to arrange that drinks should be brought to the two carriages, and with them some rather unappetising sandwiches, which Clotilda refused.

As soon as they were alone, she said to the Marquis,

"I am finding this journey far more uncomfortable than the Bay of Biscay!"

The Marquis laughed.

"It is certainly not a primrose path, but I am confident as you are such a good sailor, it will not make you sick."

She did not answer and as she sipped the wine, which the Marquis thought was of very poor quality, she looked up at him, her eyes very large in her pale face before she said,

"In case I do not have a chance to do so later I want to thank you for being so kind to me."

"Now, you are making me embarrassed," he replied, "and if I was not friendly at first, it was because I did not understand."

"But you do now?"

"You know I am wishing you every possible happiness."

She looked away from him and he knew without her saying anything that she thought that was impossible.

"Try to make a life of your own," he said. "I am sure amongst the people of Bãlutik there will be many charming and sympathetic women, and perhaps men, with whom you can be friends."

"That is what I hope," Clotilda said in a low voice, "but the Baroness admitted when I pressed her that nearly everybody at Court is German, and the Bãlutikians feel oppressed by the German atmosphere. They also find it insulting that they are not allowed to speak their own language."

"Perhaps that is something you will be able to change," the Marquis suggested.

As he spoke, he thought it very unlikely, seeing how young Clotilda was and the age of Prince Fredrick, that she would be able to alter anything.

He felt a feeling of helplessness sweep over him as for the first time in his life he was confronted with a problem to which there seemed to be no solution. It was a situation he disliked intensely.

Once again, the procession set off.

"We shall arrive at the Castle where we are staying, if all goes well, at about three o'clock," the Major said. "A large dinner has been arranged to take place early, so His Royal Highness thought there would be no point in us stopping for long on the roadway."

"I imagine we shall be quite hungry by then," the Marquis said dryly.

"There are sandwiches and wine available for both Her Ladyship and Your Lordship whenever you want them."

There was a note in the Major's voice that suggested a reproof to the Marquis for being so weak as to require sustenance on an official journey.

But the Marquis merely stretched his legs out as far as he could in front of him and closed his eyes.

He told himself that the Queen's punishment was certainly beginning to strike home and he was glad Her Majesty did not have the satisfaction of knowing how much he was disliking the journey and what lay at the end of it.

It was impossible for him not to be aware that sitting beside him Clotilda was tense, and although she said very little, there was an expression of apprehension in her eyes.

'Why the hell did I ever get mixed up in all this?' he asked himself.

Then he remembered that it was all due to the duel he had fought over Sheila Castleton, though for the moment he found it hard to remember even what she looked like.

On and on the horses plodded, the wheels lurching over stones, and as they moved higher the land on either side of the road seemed rougher and more isolated than it had been before.

Then, when they were all silent and everybody in the carriage seemed to be half-asleep, there was the sudden sound of a rifle shot, and as the Marquis opened his eyes, it was followed by another.

It was so unexpected that for a moment nobody moved.

Then the Officer, who was in charge of the troops, jumped out on one side of the carriage and the Major on the other.

But as the Marquis was about to follow them, he saw the Major stagger back against the carriage and he thought he had been shot in the arm.

It was then he remembered Clotilda and how frightened she would be, and putting his arm around her he pulled her down onto the floor.

Even as he did so a bullet shattered the window and the glass sprayed out all over them.

"What is happening? Who is shooting at us?" Clotilda cried.

"I have no idea," the Marquis replied. "I gather His Royal Highness has made a number of enemies in this part of the world, which is why we have been moving through it in such a surreptitious manner."

As he spoke, he could hear the Officer who had been in their carriage shouting orders.

This was followed by a loud volley of shots.

Suddenly there was the sound of women screaming, and the Marquis thought that it must come from the cart loaded with boys and girls who were still behind.

He made a movement as if to rise from the floor, but Clotilda put out her hands to hold on to him.

"Do not leave me," she begged.

"No, of course not," he answered. "I am sure it is just a skirmish and, as you know, we have enough soldiers to protect us."

There was more shooting, then an ominous silence, until suddenly, so that they both started, the door of the carriage was pulled open.

As the Marquis looked up and slowly raised himself back onto the seat, he was aware who their assailants were.

Facing him were two men, whom he would have known anywhere in the world without being told, that they were brigands.

Dressed in shaggy sheepskin coats over clothes that had some resemblance to Albanian national dress, they both wore a wide belt holding knives and pistols.

Each brigand had a rifle slung over his shoulder as well as a pistol in his hand.

In a language that was impossible to understand they told the Marquis and Clotilda to get out of the carriage, but their gestures made it obvious what they required.

Because it was impossible to do anything but obey, the Marquis stepped out onto the stony road and put out a helping hand towards Clotilda.

Then, as he looked around, he was appalled by what he saw.

There were thirty or forty brigands, some of them standing on the road, others above it on a vantage point from which it had been easy to ambush the cavalcade.

The coachman driving their carriage had been wounded, and a number of soldiers who appeared to be dead, were lying on the ground while the carriage that had contained Havers and Greta and the baggage was being ransacked.

A dozen brigands were dragging the trunks onto the ground and forcing them open with their sharp knives, throwing out the contents while searching, the Marquis was aware, for anything that they considered valuable.

He took everything in with a quick glance, then saw that the cart which had brought up the rear of the procession containing the young people had been overturned.

The girls and boys, looking very frightened, were being marshalled into a group at the side of the road.

It was a terrifying sight, and he was not surprised when Clotilda holding on to his arm with both hands, asked in a frightened whisper.

"W-what shall we do?"

"There is nothing we can do," the Marquis replied quietly. "Do you understand what they are saying?"

"N-no I expect they are Albanians. I remember Papa telling me that their brigand bands are very ferocious?"

"They certainly look it!" the Marquis muttered.

The brigands who had ordered them out of the carriage now searched it to see if there was anything of value inside before they came back to them.

They pointed to the Marquis's watch and chain, which he handed over to them.

Then one of them pointed with his pistol at Clotilda's neck and she quickly took off the gold pendant that had been a wedding present and which she had thought would look rather pretty with her new gown.

The Marquis was made to turn out his pockets, and a purse with golden sovereigns went into a brigand's pocket, besides a scarf pin in the shape of a diamond horseshoe.

Then as they seemed to wait for their orders, walking slowly down the hillside came their leader.

It was obvious from the way every brigand's head turned in his direction who he was, and he was actually a very fine figure of a man.

He was also extremely frightening.

He had a long, curly moustache and thick dark hair, and an air about him that was one of immense authority. When he spoke his voice was deep and resonant and seemed to ring out as if each word were a clarion call.

He gave his orders first to the brigands in charge of the young people. He had obviously ordered them up the mountain, because they were forced to climb off the road up a rough, steep track.

Then the brigand chief walked with an air of arrogance towards the pile of clothing that had been thrown out of the trunks.

Clotilda saw her new gowns, which had cost so much money and had been chosen with such care by the Countess, chucked to one side into the dust while the brigands held up with delight her wedding presents.

The silver *entrée* dishes glinted in the sun and obviously impressed them, and on the brigand chief's instructions they were thrust into a sack.

They also seemed to be intrigued by the Marquis's dressing case, having hacked their way through the crocodile leather, not bothering to have it unlocked.

Now they pulled out the gold-backed hairbrushes and bottles with gold tops, waving them excitedly in the air.

Greta was holding on to a small case that contained Clotilda's jewels.

There were not many, but the brigands were delighted with the diamond brooch that her uncle and aunt had given her, and the few trinkets she had collected from other relations.

The brigand chief then gave orders as to where they were to be taken, and with them went Havers and Greta, who gave an agonised look towards the Marquis and Clotilda before they were taken away.

"Where are they going? What will happen to them?" Clotilda asked.

"I have no idea," the Marquis replied, "and there is nothing we can do but keep quiet."

By this time the brigand chief had reached the carriage that contained the Baroness.

Clotilda had been upset that she was travelling with no other woman but was escorted only by two of the junior Officers who had come in charge of the soldiers.

Both of them were very young and had reached only the rank of Lieutenant.

One of them was standing outside the carriage, while the other, who had obviously gone to the brake containing the soldiers, was lying on the ground wounded in the leg.

The brigand looked into the carriage and Clotilda thought he could understand that the Baroness was too old to get out as they had obviously ordered her to do.

Then as he just stood there staring inside, she had a sudden fear that something terrible had happened.

"Do you think the shock of the shooting on top of the journey has been too much for her?" she said.

At the urgency of her voice the Marquis would have moved towards the carriage behind them, but the two brigands who were in charge of them threatened him with their pistols.

There was therefore nothing he could do until the brigand chief came sauntering up to them.

He looked at the Marquis in a hostile manner.

"Do you understand me?" said the Marquis in German.

There was no response, and as she understood what he was doing, Clotilda asked the same question, first in Serbian, then Romanian and finally Bãlutik.

The brigand chief obviously did not understand, or else did not wish to.

He merely shook his head and gave an order to the other two brigands, who motioned to them to walk ahead, prodding them in the back with their pistols.

"I must see to the Baroness, I must see if I can do anything for her," Clotilda said.

The Marquis pointed to the carriage behind theirs, and miming quite eloquently with his hands, asked if they could go and look at the Baroness.

The brigand chief understood.

He said just one word, and although neither Clotilda nor the Marquis understood it, they both knew what he meant.

The Baroness was dead.

"She told me her heart was weak and had been giving her pain ever since she had been so ill in the Bay of Biscay," Clotilda said in a low voice.

She put her hand in the Marquis's as she spoke and he said quietly,

"She was very old. She ought never to have been sent on the journey, but I am sure she did not suffer. A heart attack can be very quick and merciful."

"She insisted on coming with us today."

"I do not think anything you could have said would have had any effect," the Marquis replied. "She had Prince Fredrick's orders, and she had every intention of carrying them out."

As he spoke, he remembered he had seen the Major wounded on the other side of the carriage from which they had alighted.

He looked back but could not see him from where they were standing.

As there were a great number of brigands moving amongst the carriages and taking the horses from between the shafts, he supposed that something sooner or later would be done about the wounded.

In the meantime, he was mainly concerned with not annoying the brigand who held a pistol to the small of his back.

It was a very steep climb uphill for Clotilda, though the Marquis, who was in very good athletic shape, did not find it any more exhausting than did the brigands, who clambered over the stones and rough ground, he thought, like monkeys.

They climbed for quite a distance until when they reached the top of the rising ground, they saw to their surprise ahead of them a large white building.

It did hot look in the least like a brigand stronghold, and a second glance told the Marquis it was in fact a monastery.

Clotilda, who had travelled so much that she was aware of the same thing, said in a frightened voice,

"Y-You do not think they have killed the Monks?"

"I very much doubt it," the Marquis answered. "As they are a large band, there is certain to be a number of Catholics amongst them."

"Y-Yes of course," she agreed with a little sigh of relief, "and if there are monks here, we could ask them to bury the Baroness."

"I only hope we can speak their language?"

"I am so annoyed that I cannot speak Albanian," Clotilda whispered. "Papa could, but I never bothered to learn it."

"We can only pray there will be somebody more civilised when we reach the monastery."

It took them another ten minutes to get there, and as they went in through an open door into a large, enclosed courtyard, the Marquis was certain that if the Brigands had not killed the monks, they had certainly taken over the monastery.

This was confirmed when he heard the brigand chief, who had walked jauntily ahead of them as if leading in the spoils of war, stopped at the entrance to the courtyard and gave a great shout.

It must have been a cry for attention, because two or three very old monks in white habits appeared as if in reply to his order.

They could obviously understand his language, for he talked to them for some minutes, gesticulating as he spoke in the direction from which he had come.

"Surely he is asking them to attend to the wounded?" Clotilda said.

"I expect so," the Marquis replied, "but instead of worrying about them, we must worry about us, and try to find somebody to whom we can speak."

By this time the courtyard was filled up, first with the young people from Drina who were all squeezed together in one corner, the girls holding on to each other in a frightened manner.

On the other side were the soldiers who had not been wounded. They had been deprived of their arms and also for some reason their helmets.

They stood sheepishly, looking rather ashamed of themselves, and the only Officer with them was the young Lieutenant who had survived unscathed.

As the Marquis looked around, he saw that Havers and Greta had been brought in and were standing separately, as if there were no particular group to which they belonged.

Then as the brigands carrying the spoils from the luggage began to arrive laden like the tinkers whom Clotilda had seen at the country fairs, with silver dishes, gold brushes, inkpots and toast racks, the Marquis said in a loud and resonant voice,

"I wish to speak to the Abbot in charge of this monastery?"

Because it was so unexpected, everybody turned to look at him.

The brigand chief had a scowl on his face as he walked towards the Marquis.

Clotilda had a sudden fear that he might strike him, and she moved a little closer to lay both her hands on the Marquis's arm.

The brigand chief stopped and, instead of looking at the Marquis, he looked at her.

He stared at her as if he were surprised by what he saw. Then there was a very different expression on his face to what there had been before.

Because instinctively she knew he was dangerous, she moved even closer to the Marquis than she was already.

Then to her consternation the brigand chief put out his hand as if to touch her.

As he did so, onto the steps in front of a large door at the end of the courtyard came a monk.

Afterwards the Marquis was to think that he would never know a man with such a commanding personality and unmistakable magnetism, so that he compelled those he met to listen to him.

The Abbot was very old, and yet from the moment he appeared a strange hush fell over the people gathered in the courtyard, and it was impossible to look at anybody except him.

Even the brigand chief turned round, and as he did so the Marquis acted.

He walked swiftly across the courtyard and stood at the bottom of the steps, and judging from the Abbot's appearance that he was Italian by race, he said,

"Reverend Father, I am the Marquis of Weybourne, and I have come from England to represent Her Majesty Queen Victoria and the Prince Consort at the wedding."

Before he could say more the Abbot put his finger to his lips in the age-old gesture of one who commands silence.

Then speaking in such a low voice that only the Marquis could hear him, he said in Italian,

"Say no more. It is dangerous!"

Raising his voice again he spoke in Albanian, and it was obvious from his tone that he was telling the brigands what he intended to do.

Then he said to the Marquis and Clotilda,

"Come with me?"

He walked ahead of them as he spoke through the open door, and following him they found themselves in a quiet, cool refectory, and passing through it came to some cloisters out of which Clotilda could see the open door of the Chapel.

The Abbot opened a door, and they followed him into a small room in which there were a desk, several chairs, and on the wall a large crucifix.

The Marquis shut the door behind them, and the Abbot beckoned them to sit down on two of the wooden chairs while he seated himself at his desk.

"Now, my children," he said quickly, in Italian, "you must understand that you are in a very precarious position."

"I understand that we have been apprehended in order to obtain a ransom," the Marquis replied, "and I am perfectly prepared to pay a large sum for the lady with me and the other members of our party."

"That of course is expected," the abbot said, "but let me beg of you not to say, which I suspect to be the case, that the lady by your side is the chosen bride of Prince Fredrick of Bãlutik."

"You are aware of that?" the Marquis asked.

'I myself am aware of it," the Abbot answered, "but the brigands who have just held you up arrived only last night from the South."

"So it was not their intention to halt a wedding procession?" the Marquis exclaimed.

"I think they have no idea that anything unusual is happening in Bãlutik or anywhere else in this part of the world."

"And you say it would be dangerous for me to announce who I am," the Marquis said, "and that this lady is to be the bride of His Royal Highness?"

"The answer to that is quite simple," the Abbot replied. "There are, I am certain, one if not two anarchists in the brigand band who are wanted by the police for crimes in various parts of Europe."

Clotilda gave a little cry of fear.

She knew that anarchists wished to destroy monarchs wherever they could find them and were quite indiscriminating as to which country they ruled.

"I understand," the Marquis said after a moment, "and I can only beg of you, Reverend Father, to help us, if you can."

"I will do that, if it is God's will," the Abbot replied, "but I can assure you it is very difficult."

As if he thought he should explain, he went on.

"Last night the brigands walked into the monastery and announced that we were all their prisoners, but because we were Holy men, and of course unarmed, they would not hurt us so long as we did as we were told."

"Could you please, Reverend Father, find out if the Baroness who is accompanying me as my Lady-in-Waiting has died of a heart attack, as we think," Clotilda interrupted quickly. "And if she is dead, could you please bury her?"

"I promise you, my child, that the dead will be buried, and the wounded attended to. I have already told the brigands they are to bring everybody up to the monastery as quickly as possible, and in that, if in nothing else, they will obey me."

"Now, about the ransom," the Marquis said. "I think, although I do not understand Albanian, they told you that was what you were to arrange."

There was a faint smile on the old Abbot's face as he said,

"The brigands are well-aware you cannot speak their language, My Lord. I therefore told them that as you are obviously rich, I would extort the largest sum of money possible as long as they gave ten percent of the ill-gotten gains to God."

"That was exceedingly intelligent of you," the Marquis smiled. "It will make them feel sure that in those circumstances you will demand as much as possible."

"That is what I thought," the Abbot replied, "but I have something very unpleasant to tell you."

"What is it?" the Marquis asked.

The Abbot paused for a moment, as if he were trying to find words. Then he said,

"We have many different bands of brigands in Albania, as I expect you know, but these, who are more intelligent and therefore more avaricious, have entered into a very unsavoury pact with the Turks."

The Marquis looked surprised.

He knew that all those who lived in the Balkans resented the way it had been overrun by the Ottoman Empire, and the majority of the Balkan people hated the Turks and everything to do with them.

"You may remember," the Abbot went on as the Marquis did not speak, "that after the Napoleonic Wars the Barbary pirates on the coast of Africa, who preyed on shipping, captured a large number of hostages for whom huge ransoms were extorted. They also made a great deal of additional money by selling young women who were virgins to the sultan of Turkey!"

The Marquis stiffened and stared at the Abbot as if he could hardly believe what he had heard.

"Evil casts a long shadow," the Abbot went on, "and is seldom forgotten."

"Are you telling me, Reverend Father," the Marquis asked in a voice he found it hard to control, "that these Brigands are doing the same thing?"

"Yes, but the young women in this case do not have to travel farther than to the Turks in Macedonia," the Abbot replied, "who pay very large sums for them."

"I cannot believe it!" the Marquis exclaimed.

"I assure you that this is unfortunately the truth."

"Then of course the only thing we can do," the Marquis said quickly, "is to swear that Lady Clotilda is my wife?"

There was a little pause before the Abbot answered.

"*You* may be prepared to swear it, my son, but I hope you will understand that as a man of God, I cannot tell a lie!"

CHAPTER SIX

There was a tense silence while the Marquis digested what the Abbot had said.

Then he felt a very cold, trembling hand slip into his.

He turned his head slowly and looked down into Clotilda's eyes, which were pleading with him.

With a faint smile on his lips as if he were somehow amused at the way events were shaping themselves, he said,

"I must ask you, Reverend Father, if you will marry me to Lady Clotilda immediately."

"That is what I thought you would say, My Lord," the Abbot replied, "but such a marriage is not completely valid unless one of you was baptised as a Catholic."

The Marquis felt Clotilda's fingers tremble again in his before she said,

"I was baptised when I was born because I arrived unexpectedly when my mother was staying in my grandmother's house in Romania. Thinking I would not live, my grandmother sent for a Priest."

She paused, then aware that both men were listening to her intently she went on.

"When later we all returned to England I was, on the insistence of my grandfather, the Duke, christened in the Parish Church, where all my ancestors are buried."

"Then as far as I am concerned you are a Catholic," the Abbot said gently. "Therefore, my children, there is no time to lose. Come with me?"

He rose as he spoke and opened a door on the other side of the room, which led directly into the Chapel.

It was small, quiet, and dimly lit, but somehow right in its austerity.

The sanctuary lamp was flickering before the altar and the Abbot, after genuflecting, motioned to Clotilda and the Marquis to kneel down in front of him.

It was a short service, and when the Marquis repeated his vows in a strong, resonant voice, Clotilda thought hers in comparison sounded very weak and frightened.

At the same time her heart was singing in a strange manner, and she felt as if, so long as she held on to the Marquis, she was safe not only from the brigands, but also from everything that had terrified her since leaving England.

The Marquis put his signet ring, which surprisingly the brigands had overlooked, on her finger. The Abbot blessed them, then knelt in prayer before he led the way back into his sitting room.

Then, as they seated themselves in front of him as they had done before, he said in a matter-of-fact voice that was very different from the one he had used in the sanctity of the Chapel,

"Now, My Lord, what do you suggest I offer as a ransom for you and your wife?"

"I leave it to you, Reverend Father," the Marquis replied, "and I suppose they realise the difficulty there will be in obtaining ready cash."

The Abbot nodded as if he also thought of that, and the Marquis went on.

"I can give them a 'note of hand' to a Bank in Athens or Naples, whichever they prefer, and I suppose we shall have to remain here as their prisoners until some kind of courier can return with their ill-gotten gains."

"I am sure that will be obligatory," the Abbot agreed.

"And now I suggest," the Marquis replied, "although of course I am prepared to go higher, that you offer them 5,000 pounds for my wife and myself, and another 1,000 if they allow my valet to wait on us."

He paused before he added,

"I am hoping we can be housed somewhere where we can have some privacy and that we do not have to share with other people."

"I had thought of that," the Abbot said, "and if you will wait here, I will see, My Lord, whether I can get them to agree."

He rose as he spoke and left the room, leaving the Marquis and Clotilda alone.

There was a little silence before the Marquis said in a calm voice,

"I am sure when we are free it will be possible for our marriage to be annulled because of the circumstances in which it was forced upon us."

Clotilda did not reply. She only turned her head away as if she did not wish the Marquis to look at her.

As he did not speak again, she said after a moment,

"I-I am sorry."

"Why should you apologise?" the Marquis asked. "The person who has behaved disgracefully is Prince Fredrick. He should have sent more soldiers to protect you and should have had the route guarded so that the brigands could not surprise us in such an outrageous manner."

He spoke angrily as he thought of the lives that had been lost and the chaos the brigands had been able to inflict.

Then he knew without her saying so that Clotilda was irrepressibly glad that she now did not have to go on to Bãlutik to marry the Prince.

As if she thought her relief was perhaps too optimistic, she turned impulsively to the Marquis and asked,

"The Reverend Father was not mistaken? Now I am married, they will not take me to Macedonia?"

"I am sure that you are safe as my wife," the Marquis said quietly.

It seemed a long time before the Abbot returned.

When he came in, the Marquis knew as soon as he saw the faint smile on the old man's face that he had been successful.

"The brigands have agreed," he said as he reached their side, "and they will send two men immediately with your 'note of hand' to Athens. Only when they return will you be allowed to go free."

"You do not think they will break their word?" the Marquis asked.

He looked intently at the Abbot as he spoke, and both men knew they were thinking more of Clotilda than of the freedom that could be bought with the ransom.

"I know they intend to keep it," the Abbot said, "but if they move South to meet their messengers on their return, you may have to go with them."

The Marquis frowned and the Abbot said,

"In the meantime, I have arranged for you to stay in my custody in a place that I myself and sometimes my monks use when we fast in solitary confinement."

Clotilda looked apprehensive and the Marquis felt her put her hand in his as they followed the Abbot to walk slowly across the room into the cloisters.

There was a door at the side of the monastery and the Marquis saw that some distance away from the main building there was what appeared to be a small stone hut.

When they reached it, walking over rough ground to do so, they found it consisted of two rooms, one of which was a bedroom, the other containing only a *prie-dieu* in front of a large crucifix, a table and a chair.

"It is not very comfortable," the Abbot admitted, "but at least you will be alone here."

"That is more important than anything else," the Marquis said, "and we can only express our deep gratitude."

"Thank you," Clotilda said, "thank you, Father. But I am worried about Greta, my maid who looked after me on the ship."

"As she is older than the other women for whom the brigands have plans," the Abbot replied, "she is at the moment helping to nurse the wounded. There are quite a number of them, and my monks are old I think therefore you would be wise not to enquire after her or let the brigands think she is of any importance to you."

"Yes, of course," Clotilda agreed.

"I have also arranged," the Abbot said, "that as it is a long way to bring your food, your valet shall wait on you, and they have agreed to this as long as his ransom is raised to 2,000 pounds."

"But I am only too willing to do it," the Marquis said.

He sat down as he spoke at the plain table and, drawing some papers from the inner pocket of his coat, wrote out clearly a 'note of hand' to a Bank in Athens for the sum of 7,000 pounds.

He thought as he did so that he would be prepared to pay a great deal more to be free of men who he was sure would commit any crime that brought them wealth and were in the full sense of the word 'outlaws' from every civilised country.

"There is one thing more," the Abbot said. "I have given the brigands my assurance that you will not try to escape. Actually, it would be quite impossible to do so. At the same time, unless you wish to have your feet chained together or be subjected to other humiliations, I know I can trust you to keep your word."

"You can certainly do that, Reverend Father," the Marquis agreed.

"As I have said," the Abbot smiled, "to attempt to escape would endanger your lives and also prove an impossibility. Let me show you why."

He went out through the door they had just entered and walked a little way towards where in the distance they could see the sea.

He stopped, and when the Marquis and Clotilda came to his side he pointed downwards.

They saw they were standing on the very brink of a deep gorge.

It seemed to Clotilda there was a drop of thousands of feet and then she saw it was a strange inlet of the sea which came right up to this point of the mountainside.

The Abbot smiled at her surprise and said,

"This is known as Devil's Gorge, and I assure you quite a number of people have lost their lives trying to climb it."

"I can promise you with all sincerity that is something we shall not attempt," the Marquis said.

They walked back to the little house and the Abbot blessed them again before he returned to the monastery.

As he did so the Marquis saw that there was a high wall running from the far end of the building to the edge of the gorge and another on the other side of the monastery, which he was certain cut them off from reaching the route by which they had come by road.

He could understand the walls were there to make the monks feel more secure from intrusion and the curiosity of passers-by.

But it meant that even if they had not given their word of honour, it would be very difficult to escape, and it would be easy for the brigands to prevent anybody from leaving the monastery except by the main door.

He did not say anything of this to Clotilda, who was looking at the one small bed, the Marquis thought, with an expression of dismay on her face.

Because he could guess what she was thinking, he said in a conversational tone,

"If you are worried about my being uncomfortable, I am sure Havers, who prides himself on being able to cope with every possible crisis, even one like this, will find me something on which to sleep. And I have a feeling that your mattress, if it is not filled with nails, will certainly be as hard and uncomfortable as the floor."

Clotilda laughed. Then she said,

"H-How could we have expected for one moment that this would happen to us? And think of all those poor soldiers being k-killed!"

There was a little tremor in her voice, and the Marquis was afraid that now as the first shock was over, she would react to the horror of what they had seen when they stepped from the carriage.

"I think," he said, "we have to count our blessings, and as perhaps we shall be counting them for some time, we must think of new ideas and new subjects to occupy our minds."

"That is just the sort of thing Papa would have said," Clotilda answered, "a-and I am sure that is very sen-si-ble."

She stammered a little over the last word as if she were not far from tears.

Then with what the Marquis knew was a great effort at self-control she took off her bonnet and her travelling cloak and laid them down on the bed.

Reading her expression, he knew she was thinking first of the Baroness, then of the young girls whom the brigands would take to Macedonia.

Because he was worried about her reaction he said,

"Now, Clotilda, I am going to see how proficient you are in making a home out of what is little bigger than a box After all, it should not be so difficult when you have had the experience of coping with a tent in the desert, a cave in the mountains, and perhaps on other occasions nothing more than the shade of a tree?"

"You are quite right," Clotilda answered. "I am sure that if it rains at least the roof we have at the moment will protect us, which is more than Papa and I had once. The rushes overhead not only let in the rain, but also a large number of very unpleasant insects and lizards!"

The Marquis laughed, knowing that he had taken her past what might have been an emotional moment and told himself it was something he might have to do a great many times in the future.

It was a half hour later when Havers appeared and when he came, he was carrying one of Clotilda's trunks.

He put it down on the ground and they saw that the leather lid had been cut open by the brigands and Havers had piled into it some of the clothes that had been flung out in their search for treasure.

Clotilda's pretty gowns from Bond Street and the Marquis's clothes from Savile Row were all mixed up together.

There were shoes and night attire, stockings and breeches, in one untidy mess. At the same time, they had at least been saved from destruction.

"'Ere's a nice kettle o' fish, and no mistake, My Lord!" Havers said.

Because it was just the sort of thing he would say in such circumstances, the Marquis laughed.

"You have certainly been clever, Havers," he said, "in bringing us something to wear, if nothing else."

"I'm only hopin', My Lord, I can get you something to eat," Havers replied. "Them brigands are roastin' an ox in the centre of the courtyard, but I doubts if when it's cooked it'd be somethin' Her Ladyship'd fancy?"

"We will have to be content with anything you can find us," the Marquis replied.

"That's true, My Lord," Havers agreed, "but I'll have to be careful not to offend 'em. When one of the soldiers argued with one of the dirty robbers just now, he nearly 'ad his 'and cut off?"

Clotilda gave a little cry of horror, and Havers said,

"Now, don't you worry yourself, My Lady. I've been smarmin' up to them and there's one who can speak French, and he and I've got along fine. In fact, 'e helped me with the clothes, and 'e's found a room, or I s'pose you'd call it a cell, in the monastery where he's put a lot of other things."

He looked round the small house disparagingly and said,

"There's not much room in 'ere for wardrobes."

The way he spoke made Clotilda laugh.

Their supper consisted of some soup, which was what the monks themselves had for their evening meal, slices of coarse black bread and goat's cheese.

Both Clotilda and the Marquis were so hungry that they ate everything Havers brought them.

When they had finished, and it did not take long, Clotilda said,

"We must pretend we are enjoying something delicious that your chef has cooked for you in London or in your house in the country, and you are drinking the finest claret or, if you prefer, champagne."

"I doubt if my imagination will stretch that far," the Marquis said dryly.

"You will have to try," she said firmly. "Otherwise you will become so disagreeable after a few days here that I shall be as afraid of you as I was when you first came aboard the ship at Tilbury!"

"I have apologised for that."

"Yes, I know, and I thank God every second that you are with me and I am not alone."

She clasped her hands together as she went on.

"Can you imagine what it would have been like if you had not been sent to represent the Queen and the Prince Consort?"

The expression in her eyes was very eloquent and the Marquis said,

"I am sure we can attribute it all to fate, or perhaps your prayers have been answered in a very strange manner."

He thought as he spoke that he had asked for a miracle to save Clotilda from going to Bãlutik, but if this was the reply, it was certainly one he had not expected.

Although he did not say so, he could not help thinking that when the Prince heard what had happened, which he was bound to do by tomorrow, he would send a strong military force to rescue his bride.

He was afraid that then the brigands would move away, taking their prisoners with them.

It was a thought that worried him considerably, but he had no intention of mentioning it to Clotilda.

So he tried to agree to her fantasies as to what they should think about food, or a little while later their plans for tonight.

"I suppose the best thing would be for us to take turns in sleeping on the bed and do it in 'watches' as they do aboard ship," Clotilda suggested.

The Marquis smiled.

"I feel I should play the gentleman, and say I am perfectly satisfied with the floor."

He knew as he spoke that it had never crossed Clotilda's mind for one moment that now they were married they could share the small bed.

He supposed, although he was not certain, that she was remembering his saying it would be possible to get the marriage annulled and had therefore assumed they would behave just as impersonally as they had on the ship.

He had, however, not allowed for the ingenuity of Havers.

After their meagre supper was finished the valet arrived carrying a mattress on his back and a blanket and a pillow.

He put the mattress down on the floor after pushing the *prie-dieu* to one side and said,

"There y'are, My Lord. It ain't made o' goose feathers but it's better than nothing?"

"It certainly is," the Marquis agreed, "and I think it extremely clever of you to have obtained it for me."

"I got it off o' the monks," Havers said. "Nice old chap, as thinks it'll be good for 'is soul to give up the comforts of the body?"

"Do you mean to say this is his mattress?" the Marquis asked.

"I persuaded 'im, My Lord, that your need was greater than 'is." Havers said.

Having said goodnight to Havers, the Marquis said to Clotilda,

"I know of no one I would rather have with me in a tight spot than Havers! He always pops up smiling, and nothing defeats him."

"I am aware of that, and I think he is wonderful?"

Clotilda looked as she spoke at one of her beautiful lace-trimmed nightgowns that the Countess had bought her in Bond Street, which was lying ready for her on the bed.

There was also the Marquis's nightshirt laid out neatly on the mattress in the same way that it would have been if they were at home in England.

Then she laughed.

"What are you laughing at?" the Marquis asked.

"I am thinking if Havers is fantastic, you are too," she said, "to have such an extraordinary, resourceful valet. I used to look after Papa when Mama was no longer with us, but I was not nearly so efficient."

"I am efficient enough to realise that you are at this moment rather tired," the Marquis said. "You have had a long and frightening day, so go to bed, Clotilda. Tomorrow we will try to think of ways of amusing ourselves so that, as you say, I do not become disagreeable."

He was teasing her, but Clotilda's expression was very serious as she said,

"I want to thank you for being so kind and for looking after me. If you were not here, I think I would want to jump into Devil's Gorge."

"You are not to say such things," the Marquis objected, "because I can only commend you, Clotilda, for being the bravest woman I have ever met."

"Brave?" Clotilda exclaimed in astonishment.

The Marquis was aware that any other woman of his acquaintance would have been screaming, crying and clinging to him, not only during the shooting but afterwards, when they had seen so many people dead or wounded.

And all the more when they had been made prisoners by the brigands.

Most young women, he knew, would have been hysterical at the thought of being sold to some Turk in Macedonia because she was a virgin.

But Clotilda's behaviour had been exemplary, and it had made him aware of what a very unusual and commendable person she was, apart, he thought, from the fact that she was very beautiful.

As he looked at her, he thought she glowed almost like a light in the small, austere building that might have been a marble niche for a Saint, which he was beginning to think she was.

Then as he looked into her large eyes and was aware of the soft curves of her breasts beneath her fashionable gown, he knew she was also very much a woman.

Abruptly he turned away from her to say,

"Go to bed, Clotilda! If you want me, you have only to call and I shall hear you. I too am tired."

She went to her bedroom and, closing the door, began to take off her gown.

By now the sun had set in a blaze of glory and the stars were coming out in the sky above.

There were no curtains over the windows and Clotilda did not light the one candle that stood on a small stool by her bed.

There was nowhere to put her gown when she had taken it off except over the chair that Havers had brought in from the other room after they had finished supper.

It looked untidy with her clothes heaped in a pile on it and Clotilda thought that tomorrow she must try to make everything neater.

'I am sure the Marquis is very fastidious,' she thought.

It was however difficult to think what she could do with the clothes that were still stuffed into the trunk.

She put on her nightgown and got into bed, and although it was still very warm, she was sure that later on there might be a chill wind blowing down from the mountains or from the sea.

She therefore covered herself first with a coarse cotton sheet, then with a blanket.

She had the idea that the monks would have no more warmth in the winter, and perhaps that was another penance they paid for past sins.

'They are very good men,' Clotilda thought sleepily, 'but I am glad that I do not have to be a nun.'

She knew when she had been so afraid of what was waiting for her at Bãlutik it had never crossed her mind that she might go into a convent.

She wanted to stay in the world, to meet people, to talk with them and live her life fully.

She was sure that was how the Marquis had lived, and now to think of him made her remember how kind he had been and that for the moment she was actually married to him.

'As he said, when we are free we can get an annulment,' she told herself. 'But as it now is, the brigands will not touch me.'

She shut her eyes and quickly said her prayers, hoping not to think of the brigands or the soldiers they had left dead or wounded.

She was just drifting into sleep when suddenly she was awoken by the feeling that something had moved.

As she came back to consciousness she could not imagine where she was.

Then as she opened her eyes she was sure that the room was very dark and there was not the light from the moon or the stars there had been when she got into bed.

Something in the darkness had moved and to her astonishment she realised that somebody was blocking up the whole aperture of the window.

Her skin crept and her mind could not comprehend what was happening.

Then suddenly there was the light of the sky shining behind something huge and shapeless.

It moved silently towards her, and while she still could not understand what it could be, suddenly a hand covered her mouth and a heavy weight came down on top of her, forcing the breath out of her body.

She tried to scream, but she was powerless to move or make a sound.

As a shaft of terror struck through her she felt the chief brigand, for she realised now it was he, tearing her nightgown away from her shoulders.

Then he was pulling at the blanket she had wrapped over her body.

Her terror was so intense that Clotilda, unable to move or think, could only feel despairingly that she was being killed with the weight and horror of what was happening to her.

*

The Marquis had known when Clotilda left him for her own room that he too was tired.

He was also hot, and he had an impulse to go out into the night air.

It was not only the heat of the atmosphere from which he was suffering, but a feeling as if it were difficult to think or to realise not only what they had been through, but also the difficulties they might suffer in the future.

He was still desperately afraid for Clotilda, not that she would be taken to Macedonia, but that the brigands might find an excuse to dispose of him so that she would be at their mercy.

He had not missed the way the chief brigand had looked at her in the courtyard.

He knew if he went outside the hut it would be very easy for a brigand on guard, if there were one, to shoot him on the pretext that he thought he was trying to escape.

This might well happen, despite the fact he had given his word to the Abbot that he would do no such thing.

He therefore opened the window wide and, pulling off his coat and shirt, threw them on the floor to sit only in his long trousers, looking up at the stars.

After a while there was a faint breeze coming from the sea.

He sat thinking out a plan in his mind as to how he could take care of Clotilda and whether it would be possible if the brigands did move, as he was sure they would, for him and Clotilda to stay where they were until they could obtain the ransom money.

He was almost certain it would be impossible, but it seemed to be the only way he could be sure of Clotilda's safety.

'Beautiful women are always a liability in a situation like this,' he told himself.

He knew that never in his whole life had he been in such an unpleasant situation and certainly not with anybody as young, helpless and lovely as Clotilda.

'If the worse comes to the worst,' he thought, 'I suppose I can shoot her, then myself!'

He could imagine nothing more horrifying and in any case he had no weapon of any sort and no possibility of obtaining one.

Again, he asked himself the question that had presented itself ever since he had left England.

'What can I do about Clotilda?'

He kept thinking of her until his head was beginning to nod and he knew, if he were sensible, he would lie down on his mattress and go to sleep.

Then just as he had determined to do so, he heard a slight noise in the next room.

It was only a faint scrape that might have been made by Clotilda turning over in bed, and yet, although it seemed unreasonable, it alerted him to a feeling of danger.

He thought such a thing was impossible, as they were isolated in the hut.

Then the sound came again and instinctively, because he was worrying about her, he rose to his feet.

He had taken off the slippers that Havers had brought to him after removing his boots, which he had been wearing for travelling, and he thought as he walked barefooted to the communicating door that he was moving so quietly that he would not wake her.

Very cautiously he turned the handle and gently pulled open the door.

The starlight made it easy to see the contents of the tiny room, and then he thought there must be something wrong with his eyes, for he saw a dark and sinister outline on the bed.

Then he was aware that a man was pulling away from under him the sheet and blanket that covered Clotilda.

The Marquis, who had learned to be very quick in an emergency, did not hesitate.

He had no weapon, but he had learned the art of self-defence on his travels.

In one stride he had reached the bed and struck violently with the base of his right hand hard as steel on the back of the brigand's neck, as he bent over Clotilda.

It was a blow that the Marquis delivered with every ounce of his considerable strength and with an expertise that would have made his instructor proud of him.

The brigand fell forward as if pole-axed and the Marquis seized him by the neck of his coat dragged him off the bed.

As the brigand's hand was relaxed from Clotilda's mouth, she made a low groan like that of a small animal in pain.

She wanted to scream very loud, but the sound would not come, and she could only watch terrified as the Marquis picked the brigand up from the floor.

Slinging him over his shoulder, he disappeared through the door and into the next room, then through the door that led outside.

It had not been locked because they had given their word of honour not to try to escape.

As he walked through it now with the brigand sprawling over his back, the Marquis thought that if they were seen, then he himself was well protected.

Aware of how heavy the brigand chief was, he could only walk slowly to the edge of Devil's Gorge.

Then with a single movement he flung the brigand's body, not caring whether he was dead or unconscious, over the side and watched in the moonlight as he fell down, down, until he reached the sea below.

Quickly, knowing it was a mistake to linger, the Marquis returned to the hut.

Clotilda was sitting on the bed, her hands over her torn nightgown.

He saw that her eyes were dark and dilated with fear, and because she did not speak or seem to notice his return, he knew that she was numb with the shock of what had happened.

He shut the door and came to sit down on the side of the bed beside her.

"It is all right," he said quietly, "he will not trouble you again."

She did not answer, and he said gently,

"Shall I get you something to drink? I think there is some water in the next room."

He made as if to move, then her hands went out towards him, and he understood that she wanted to hold on to him and was afraid of his leaving her.

He put his arms around her and held her against him, saying,

"It was very frightening for you, but he is dead now. Do you understand, Clotilda? He is dead! I have thrown him into the gorge."

It was then she gave a shudder and putting her face against his bare shoulder began to cry.

The Marquis tried to hold her closer, knowing that was what she wanted.

Then because it was easier and more comforting, he lay down on top of the bed beside her, and as he pulled her gently against him her tears came like a tempest, and she cried despairingly like a child who can no longer control its grief.

As she cried and cried, the Marquis thought that after all she had been through it was washing away some of the horror that must have been festering within her ever since she realised she was being forced to marry Prince Fredrick.

There was nothing he could do but go on holding her close. Then after a while he began to stroke the softness of her hair as it fell over her shoulders and down her back.

As her weeping began at last to subside, he realised that his naked shoulder was wet with her tears.

Her body, which had been numb and cold when he had first held her against him, was now warm, and he could feel her heart beating against his.

He did not speak. There seemed to be no need for it, but he knew without words that all she wanted was the comfort of his arms, of knowing he was there and that the terror, which had been evil and horrifying, had gone.

Only when her tears had almost ceased did the Marquis say very quietly,

"It is all right now, Clotilda?"

"B-But another m-man might c-come!" she said beneath her breath.

"I think that is very unlikely," the Marquis assured her, "but I will stay here with you if you want me to."

"D-do not leave me, please do not leave me?"

She was filled with fear again and he said,

"I will stay here for the rest of the night, so go to sleep, Clotilda. You are very tired."

"Y-you will not leave me?"

"I promise you I will not do that."

He pulled her a little closer to him, as if to reassure her, and as he did so he felt her fingers spread out across his bare chest as if to make sure he could not move without her being aware of it.

Then he knew her eyes were closed and, because she was utterly exhausted, she was falling asleep.

The Marquis smiled to himself.

He could not help wondering what his friends would think if they could see him lying there with a very beautiful girl in his arms, and both of them wearing the minimum amount of clothes.

He knew they would put a very different interpretation on the situation from what was actually the truth.

He shut his eyes.

He thought that what he felt for Clotilda was very different from anything he had felt for any other woman he had ever known in his life.

Because this emotion was so different, it was almost impossible to put it into words.

And yet he knew if he were honest that it could all be summed up in one word of four letters – *love.*

CHAPTER SEVEN

The dawn came slowly up the sky and the Marquis thought it was the same colour as Clotilda's hair, which was falling over her shoulders and against her chest.

She had not moved for a long time, but he had the idea that she was not deeply asleep and was still slightly tense in case he should leave her.

He thought he heard somebody approaching their little house and very gently moved his arm from around her.

Instantly Clotilda opened her eyes.

"What is wrong?" she asked. "What is h-happening?"

"It is all right," he said gently. "I can hear somebody coming and I expect it is Havers."

He thought it was rather early for Havers as he walked into his own room and shut Clotilda's door behind him.

Then as he opened the outer door he saw not Havers, but the Abbot.

"Reverend Father!" he exclaimed. "This is a surprise!"

"I want to speak to you, my son."

The Abbot entered the room and standing just inside the door said,

"The brigands are moving out. In fact, most of them have gone by now."

The Marquis was still. Then he asked,

"Why?"

"Apparently their chief has disappeared," the Abbot replied.

He looked intently at the Marquis as he spoke, who had the idea he suspected what had happened. But he thought it would be a mistake to admit anything and the Abbot continued.

"They are like sheep without a shepherd and quite helpless without being given proper orders. I think, too, although they have not said so, that one of the men on watch has reported that there are soldiers on the way here from the castle where you were expected to stay last night."

The Marquis had anticipated this, and he asked,

"Are my wife and I free to leave?"

"As far as I am concerned the answer is yes," the Abbot replied.

"Then I think," the Marquis said quickly, "we would be wise to return immediately to Drina and see if we can get a ship to take us to Italy."

As if he felt he should explain, he added,

"I have no wish to have to tell His Royal Highness that his bride is no longer available. That should be a job for the diplomats."

The Abbot's eyes twinkled.

"I have always been told, My Lord, that a wise General knows when to retreat!"

The Marquis laughed.

"That is what we will do, Reverend Father, and the quicker the better?"

"I will say goodbye to you when you are ready to leave," the Abbot said, and went from the hut.

The Marquis opened the door of Clotilda's room.

"What is happening?" she asked. "I heard the Abbot's voice. What did he say?"

"We are free – and we are leaving immediately," the Marquis replied. "Hurry, there is no time to be lost unless you wish to explain why you should not go on to Bãlutik?"

Clotilda gave a cry of horror, and before he could even shut the door began to get out of bed.

The Marquis was dressed only a few seconds before her and as he sat down to write at the table she came through the door.

As if on cue, Havers appeared at the same moment.

"I've got a carriage waitin' for Your Lordship," he announced excitedly, "and I've got all the trunks in it with the exception of this one."

He picked up the trunk that was on the floor as he spoke and turned across the rough ground towards the monastery.

"What are you writing?" Clotilda asked curiously.

"It is a thanks offering for the Abbot, which I think will please him," the Marquis replied. "He can cash it and I shall be delighted to stop payment on the one in Athens that was extorted from us by the brigands."

He put his pen back into his pocket and held out his hand.

"Come along," he said. "Once again your prayers have been answered, because I am quite certain this is what you have been praying would happen."

He felt Clotilda's fingers fasten on his as if she were afraid she would lose him.

"You did not tell the Abbot what happened last night?" she asked in a low voice.

The Marquis shook his head.

"I have a feeling he suspects that I am in some way connected with the chief brigand's disappearance, but it would not be safe to talk unnecessarily about it."

"Of course not," Clotilda agreed.

Havers, with the trunk, was just disappearing through the door of the monastery as they followed him over the rough ground.

The Abbot was waiting for them in the courtyard, which was in an indescribable mess.

In the centre was the carcass of the ox the brigands had roasted, with the ashes beneath it still glowing.

The young people who had been herded into one corner had all vanished and they were to see them later running as fast as they could back to the security of their homes in Drina.

There were rags, paper, bits of wood, rifles and pieces of uniform lying everywhere.

There were even two sheepskin coats, as if the brigands had been so frightened they'd left hurriedly.

Through the doors opening out of the courtyard, Clotilda could see the monks tending the wounded, who were lying on mattresses on the ground.

There was however no time to linger. The Marquis gave the Abbot his thanks offering, and when he accepted it, the Abbot, in return, gave him a purse.

"There is enough money in it, My Lord, to pay your fares to Italy," he said. "I am sure you will find some kind of ship to take you there, but unless it is an English one, they will expect to be paid in cash."

"We are deeply indebted to you for your kindness and thoughtfulness," the Marquis answered.

"I will remember you both in my prayers," the Abbot replied.

He blessed them, and as they realised the need to hurry, they ran hand-in-hand from the courtyard and slowed their pace only when they reached the precarious sheep track that led down to the road.

Havers was waiting for them and the Marquis saw he had recaptured two of the horses, which the brigands had taken from between the shafts, and had opened the roof of the carriage so that he could pile in all the luggage.

It looked very strange with the box lids cut open, and frills of silk and lace of Clotilda's gowns hanging out and the sleeves of one of the Marquis's smart coats.

But at least they had some clothing with them, and Havers told them angrily that a great deal had been stolen either by the brigands or by the young people, who had snatched things up as they ran home to safety.

The Marquis however was not concerned with anything except getting away and, climbing onto the box of the carriage, he pulled Clotilda up beside him.

Then as Havers flung himself on top of the luggage he drove off.

It was impossible on the rough track to go at all fast, but at least they were moving, since the route was all downhill, more quickly than they had on the way up.

The horses too were impatient to get back to their comfortable stables, and doubtless, the Marquis thought, had been left unfed except for the grass that was very sparse at the side of the road.

Ahead of and far below them was the sea, and behind the advancing Bãlutik troops, who by now would have been alerted to the fact that as their distinguished visitors had not arrived last night, there must have been trouble on the way.

As the Marquis had said to the Abbot, he had no wish to explain the circumstances that now made it impossible for Clotilda to take part in the Royal Marriage.

It was with a feeling of utter relief as they eventually drove into Drina that he saw there were several ships in the small harbour.

Two of them were only fishing vessels, but one was quite a sizeable Italian ship on its way home, he learned later, to Genoa.

The Captain was a warm-hearted Italian who was already appalled at having learned before their arrival that there had been trouble with brigands.

"Somebody should teach those varmints a lesson!" he said sternly, and the Marquis longed to say that was exactly what he had done.

As he was able to pay, he and Clotilda were provided with the best cabins aboard, which were not anything very luxurious, but clean and private.

They were given food and drink as the ship prepared to leave harbour immediately.

The Marquis thought it was unlikely that there was now any chance of their being stopped by the Bãlutik soldiers, the Prime Minister, the Foreign Secretary, or anybody else who would have been meeting them at the Castle.

But he was determined to take no chances of Clotilda having to go through any further ordeal that might frighten or embarrass her.

As the ship got under way, he heaved a sigh of relief and said to her,

"As you had a very disturbed night, I suggest you go below, get into bed and go to sleep. There is nothing more to worry you, and I know you must be tired."

"Actually, I am very happy," Clotilda said in a low voice.

"You can tell me about it later," the Marquis replied. "At the moment I have given you an order, and I expect you to obey me?"

She gave a little laugh, but she left him, and he sent Havers after her to see that she had everything she wanted.

Then he went up on deck to watch the ship moving into the open sea.

As he looked up at the mountains of Albania, he thought he had never had a more terrifying experience in the whole of his life.

He knew that by the mercy of God they had been saved from such horrors that it was impossible to think of them.

Then, because he too felt tired, he sat down in a deckchair and fell asleep.

*

They reached Naples at ten o'clock the next morning and it did not surprise the Marquis that Clotilda had slept for twenty-four hours.

"Shall I, My Lord, wake Her Ladyship?" Havers had asked the previous night when it was dinner time.

"Certainly not!" the Marquis replied. "Let her sleep for as long as possible."

He however took the precaution, just in case she should wake in the night and be frightened, of propping her cabin door open as well as his own.

Their cabins were adjacent and he knew if she cried out he would hear her.

However, the engines had been the only sound during the night and the Marquis rose early, eager to put into operation the plans that had come into his mind during the dark hours.

By the time Clotilda came to find him on deck, he was looking not only pleased with himself, but extremely elegant without a wrinkle in the clothes that had been so roughly treated by the brigands.

"You must forgive me," Clotilda said in an embarrassed voice. "I am ashamed of having slept so long."

"As you were utterly exhausted," the Marquis said, "it is not surprising! And now if you are ready, we can go ashore."

"Where are we going?"

"It is a surprise," he answered. "Havers has gone ahead to see that everything is prepared for us by the time we get there."

She smiled at him.

"I love nice surprises!"

"I promise you this will be very different from the unpleasant ones you had yesterday."

"I hope so."

He noticed that for the first time there was no fear in her eyes and the expression on her face was very different from the worried, apprehensive look that he had known ever since they had left England.

Clotilda stepped into an open carriage drawn by two well-fed horses and the Marquis got in beside her.

They drove away from the quay, but when she expected to climb up the road that she knew led to the main part of the city, they drove instead along the sea front.

Ahead of them she saw Vesuvius silhouetted against the blue sky and soon the road grew more beautiful with bougainvillaea and flowering geraniums, vivid patches of colour on either side of them.

Clotilda slipped her hand into the Marquis's.

"This is very exciting," she said. "At the same time will everybody be very angry with you and me because of what has happened!"

He knew she was too shy to say, "because we are married", and he merely replied,

"There will, of course, be a lot of explaining to do, but I have, as it happens, already sent a note to the British Consul in Naples to ask him to contact our Ambassador in Rome."

He thought Clotilda looked surprised and he said,

"It is their job to pour oil on troubled waters, so let us give them something to do and try not to worry about it ourselves."

Clotilda did not say any more, but only stared round her with delight until the horses turned in through a pair of ornamental gates and they were in a garden brilliant with flowers with a fountain playing in front of a white villa.

She looked questioningly at the Marquis and asked,

"Who is it we are staying with?"

"We are staying with nobody," the Marquis replied. "As it happens, this is my villa – and my mother spent the last few years of her life here."

As the carriage came to a standstill he went on.

"I have not been here for some years, but I have always been assured that it is being properly looked after and I am quite certain we shall be comfortable."

Clotilda had no doubt about that when she saw Havers standing smiling in the doorway.

"Welcome, My Lady," he said. "You'll 'ave a great deal more room 'ere than you 'ad in that pokey little hut at the monastery."

Clotilda smiled at what he was saying. At the same time, she was staring wide-eyed at the beauty of the interior of the villa.

She could see statues and urns besides a great number of other beautiful objects that she knew would have delighted her father.

The walls were cool and white and opened out onto the garden and, although the Marquis might not have been there for a long time, everything seemed to be well cared for and in perfect order.

This, she learned later, was due to the labours of the elderly couple who had served his mother and had remained to take care of the villa after she died.

Although it was at short notice, they had a delicious light luncheon on the terrace outside the dining room.

It was the Marquis who insisted that Clotilda have a glass of wine, which looked like sunshine, to celebrate their escape.

Then she looked at him and said,

"Never again will I despair or give up believing that God will not save me at the last moment."

The Marquis smiled, and she added in a low voice,

"Actually, it was you. For if you had not killed the brigand chief…"

"Do not speak of it or even think of it," the Marquis interrupted sharply. "Just think that we are free, Clotilda, and if we did not have enough faith, it is something we must remember another time."

Clotilda put down her glass.

"Another time?" she asked. "You are not suggesting that…"

As if she could not say the words that came to her lips, she rose from the table and walked down the marble steps into the sunlit garden.

She stood staring at the fountain and as the Marquis joined her, he said quietly,

"There is nothing for you to worry about."

"But there is!"

"Tell me!"

She lowered her voice before she answered.

"You said after we were married it would be possible to have it annulled but suppose, just suppose the Prince is prepared to wait for that to happen?"

The Marquis went nearer to her and took her hand in his.

Then to her surprise he took her back up the steps into the house and opened the door into a sitting room she had not yet seen.

She realised it was very lovely and knew instinctively that it had been his mother's drawing room. It seemed redolent of a woman who had loved beauty and, Clotilda thought, her son.

The Marquis shut the door.

Then as Clotilda stood at the window looking out over the flower-filled garden towards the blue of the sea, he said,

"I did not want to talk about it so soon, but because I know it is worrying you, let us get it over once and for all."

Clotilda waited for him to answer her question and the Marquis said slowly,

"I told you that I thought our marriage could be annulled, Clotilda, and if that is what you want, we can go to Rome to see the Pope and start in the Vatican the somewhat cumbersome machinery which deals with such matters."

"Do you think they will consider it?"

"They will certainly consider it, but it will take time and of course a lot of money, though that is immaterial."

"B-but eventually our marriage could be annulled?"

"If that is what you want."

Clotilda's eyes were on the sea and as she did not look at him the Marquis asked very quietly,

"Is that what you want, Clotilda?"

"I-I am thinking of you. The Baroness said you had always sworn you would never marry, and I am sure you did not want a wife thrust upon you in such circumstances."

"That is for me to decide," the Marquis replied. "What I am waiting to hear, Clotilda, is what *you* want."

There was silence and he knew she was trying to make up her mind what to reply.

He saw also that she had gone very pale and was twisting her fingers together as if she were deeply agitated.

He went a little nearer to her.

"We were married in very strange circumstances," he said, "but when we were kneeling in front of the Abbot in the Chapel, I thought it was a very sacred ceremony, and something that I shall always remember."

Clotilda was still. Then she said in a strange little voice he could hardly hear,

"W-what are you saying to me? I-I do not understand."

"I am saying," the Marquis answered, "that I thought when we were married, it was the miracle I had prayed for to save you first from the Prince and then from the brigands."

She looked up at him wildly, then suddenly, as if something snapped within her, her hands went out towards him, and she held on to the lapels of his coat.

"Let me stay with you *please* let me stay with you," she pleaded. "I am safe only when I am with you, and I am so afraid that the Prince will claim me again or if not somebody like him?"

Slowly the Marquis put his arms around her, but he did not hold her close. Instead, he looked down at her and said,

"What do I mean to you, Clotilda, besides being a safeguard against everything of which you are frightened?"

"Y-you mean everything," she replied. "Everything! You fill my whole world and without you I do not want to live!"

The last word was almost inaudible, as if she were afraid he would be angry. Then as if she could not help herself she whispered,

"I love you! Oh, please love me a little?"

It was then the Marquis's lips came down on hers and, pulling her close against him until it was almost impossible for her to breathe, he kissed her.

To Clotilda, it was as if the heavens opened and the sunshine outside suddenly enveloped the whole room with a dazzling light.

Then the light was within herself and the Marquis and she felt as if everything she had longed for and believed in was there on his lips.

He gave her not only the sun, but the moon, the stars and the flowers that filled the garden.

It was so beautiful, so perfect and at the same time so wildly exciting that she knew this was what she had always thought love would be like.

It was the love she had longed for, that she had seen between her father and mother and prayed she would one day find for herself.

Now it was hers.

As the Marquis kissed her and went on kissing her, she thought that she had reached Heaven and it would be impossible to feel any happier than she was at this moment.

The Marquis raised his head. Then he said in a voice that sounded unsteady,

"Do you really love me, Clotilda? Tell me because I want to be sure?"

"I love you! *I love you!*" Clotilda cried. "That was really why I bought the poison when we were in Naples because I knew that without you, I would only want to die!"

Then as if she felt she must be completely truthful she went on,

"But I did not realise it was love I felt until we were on that rough road and I felt as if I were being taken away from the Heaven that was you into an indescribable hell!"

The Marquis moved his lips over the softness of her cheek.

"I knew what I felt about you, my beautiful one, when I held you in my arms in the moonlight, and I desperately wanted to kiss you. It was very hard not to do so."

"Kiss me now! Please kiss me," Clotilda begged. "I am so afraid I shall wake up to find this has all been a dream."

The Marquis kissed her until once again they were enveloped by a rapture and a beauty that seemed blinding.

Then he said very gently,

"This is the time of day, my precious, when the Italians take their *siesta* – or *riposo* – and that is what I think we should do – together?"

For a moment Clotilda looked up at him wide-eyed, then as she understood she blushed and hid her face against his shoulder.

They went upstairs together to a room that was above the one they had just left and which Clotilda had already learned had been his mother's.

It was all white and silver and very cool with the sun blinds drawn down over the windows.

There was the scent of flowers and a very soft breeze blowing in from the sea.

Then as the Marquis put his arms around her it was impossible to think of anything but him.

She felt a wild excitement growing within her and she knew he was excited too, although his hands were very gentle as he undressed her.

He lifted her onto the bed, and she waited for him, lying against the soft, cool pillows until he came to her and said,

"You are quite certain, my precious, that you really love me? I feel as if I have waited an eternity for you. At the same time, I have no wish to frighten you as you have been frightened before."

Clotilda gave a little cry and put her arms around his neck.

"Nothing you could do could frighten me," she said, "and when you touch me, I feel little thrills running through me – which is something I have never felt before. It is like your kisses only different."

The Marquis drew in his breath. Then he was kissing her more passionately until the fire in him ignited a little flame within her.

He knew then that their love would carry them up into the sky, where there was no fear, only the rapture, the glory and the beauty of love.

*

"Do you realise," Clotilda asked as they were having breakfast on the balcony, "that we have been married for three whole days?"

"Most perfect days, my love," the Marquis said.

She put out her hand towards him and he raised it to his lips.

"Have I forgotten to tell you this morning," he asked, "that you look more beautiful than you did yesterday?"

"Do you really mean that? I am always so frightened that one morning you will wake up to find you are bored with me as you have been bored with all the other lovely ladies you have known in the past."

"Who has been talking to you?"

"Havers, of course!" Clotilda laughed. "He said 'I've never seen 'is Lordship look so young, and he's lost that bored look I used to watch for which means, My Lady, 'e wanted to be orf to pastures new!'"

"You are not to listen to Havers talking such nonsense," the Marquis exclaimed.

"I am sure it is the truth," Clotilda said. "At the same time, darling, please – please do not look for 'pastures new'."

"I have a feeling that everything about you is so new and so exciting," the Marquis answered, "that I shall never have time in this life to find out all there is to know about you."

"That is exactly what I want you to say," Clotilda said, "but I keep asking myself how there could ever be a man quite as wonderful as you are."

"That is exactly what I want you to think," the Marquis said as he poured himself another cup of coffee.

"Now you are being rather smug!" Clotilda teased. "At the same time, you must teach me never to bore you."

The Marquis looked at her across the table and thought it impossible that any woman could look so lovely, so alluring and so pure.

At the same time Clotilda had aroused in him emotions and sensations he had never known.

Never in his whole life had he felt for any woman what he felt for her.

It was, in a way, because she was so completely his, so much a part of himself, that he knew he could no more lose her than deliberately lose a leg or an arm, or indeed an organ that until now he had not known he possessed – his heart.

He had been very gentle and controlled when he made love to her because she was so innocent.

But because to Clotilda it had been part of the divine, it had aroused in him a spiritual ecstasy that was very different from the purely physical sensations he had known in the past.

Every day and every minute they were together he thought he grew to love her more.

As if she read his thoughts, Clotilda said,

"You know, darling, every time you kiss me, I think it impossible to be more excited or more thrilled. And yet I am wrong, for last night our love was so wonderful that I felt I was no longer human, but perhaps an angel."

"I will make sure you are human," the Marquis said with a touch of fire in his eyes.

"You had better eat your breakfast first!" Clotilda laughed.

Then, as if she could not help herself, she stretched her hand across the table to him again and as she did so Havers appeared in the window.

"What is it?" the Marquis asked.

"It's early for callers, My Lord," Havers said, "but Their Excellencies, the British Ambassador and the Ambassador for Bãlutik have arrived."

There was a little silence before the Marquis said,

"Tell Their Excellencies I will be down as quickly as possible."

"Very good, My Lord."

Havers disappeared and the Marquis looking across the table at Clotilda saw the worried look that had not been there for the past three days, was back in her eyes.

"You will tell them we are married?" she asked after a moment. "And that there is no chance of my ever being the Prince's wife?"

"Of course I will tell them!"

"Make them understand there was nothing else you could do if you were to save me and they must explain it to Her Majesty, the Queen."

"Leave it to me."

He walked round the table and put his arms about Clotilda, then drawing her to her feet held her very close against him.

He knew as her body pressed itself against his that she was trembling.

"There is nothing whatever to be frightened about," he said calmly. "You are mine, completely and absolutely, and neither God nor man shall ever take you from me."

He kissed her and her lips clung to his.

He knew then that he would fight the whole world rather than lose her and, if they were ostracised or exiled for what they had done, it would not matter, in his own words, *"a damn!"*

"I love you," he said gently.

Then he left her to go to his dressing room.

*

Ten minutes later, appearing completely at his ease, the Marquis walked unhurriedly down the stairs.

Only one of his closest friends, and of course Clotilda, would have been aware that there was something aggressive in the way he held his head and the set of his chin.

Havers had put the two gentlemen in the drawing room and had already supplied them each with a glass of the Marquis's best wine.

They rose as he entered and the British Ambassador held out his hand, saying,

"I received your message, My Lord, and came as quickly as I could. I have also brought with me His Excellency Baron von Wildenstein, who is the Ambassador for Bãlutik."

The Marquis shook hands with the Baron who said, speaking English with only a slightly guttural accent,

"I have, My Lord, very grievous news for you to impart to Lady Clotilda who, I understand, is resting here after her very unfortunate encounter with the Albanian brigands."

"Yes, Lady Clotilda is here," the Marquis admitted.

His Excellency seemed to have a little trouble finding words before he went on.

"It is with the deepest regret that I must ask you to inform Her Ladyship that her intended husband, His Royal Highness Prince Fredrick, was killed by an anarchist while on his way to investigate the monastery where his soldiers were massacred by the brigands who took you prisoner."

"The Prince has been – killed?"

The Marquis thought his voice sounded strange as he spoke.

"A bomb was thrown into His Highness's carriage as he was approaching the monastery"'.

For a moment the Marquis was stunned into silence. Then the British Ambassador said,

"I have already sent a messenger to the Queen with news of the tragedy. I know Her Majesty will be deeply perturbed, and of course, My Lord, you did the only thing possible in taking Lady Clotilda away from the monastery. I am filled with admiration by the way you managed to escape."

The Marquis felt there was no point in elaborating on that score, and merely inclined his head.

"I suppose," the Baron asked, "that Her Ladyship is not well enough to receive me so that I can express my regret and my country's commiserations over what is in effect, her bereavement."

"I am afraid not," the Marquis said firmly. "As you will understand, Lady Clotilda has been deeply shocked by what has occurred, and I feel sure it would be best for her to be kept as quiet as possible and try to forget what to both of us was an extremely unpleasant and terrifying experience."

"Indeed, it must have been," the Ambassador agreed, "but of course we have no detailed information about what occurred."

"There is very little to tell you," the Marquis said in a lofty manner. "The brigands were in great strength and had taken over the monastery before we, with what proved an inadequate escort, arrived at a point on the road that might have been made by nature for an ambush of that sort."

He looked pointedly at the Bãlutik Ambassador as he spoke, knowing he would be feeling uncomfortable at what he was hearing.

"There were, I understand," the Marquis went on, "a number of other troops waiting for us at the castle where we were to stay the night, but there was no sign of them, and I managed to get Lady Clotilda away the following morning."

He turned to the British Ambassador to say,

"I am sure, Your Excellency, that you and I hope, Her Majesty the Queen, will agree that there is nothing that can be done about Lady Clotilda until, when she is well enough, I will escort her back to England. But I must add frankly that I think it will be some time before she will be able to undertake the journey.

"Of course, of course," the Ambassador agreed. "We understand, and I am sure, here in your mother's beautiful villa, which I have admired on previous visits, she will soon recover her health and strength."

"I can only thank Your Excellency for making things as easy as possible for her."

"I will of course send a report of what has occurred to Her Majesty," the Ambassador said.

"Thank you," the Marquis replied.

He wondered with a faint smile what Her Majesty would feel when she learnt, as eventually she must, how her punishment had changed his life and brought him a happiness he had never expected to find.

Then as the Bãlutikian Ambassador finished off his wine, as if he could not bear to leave behind a single drop of anything so good, the Marquis asked,

"Have you any idea who will succeed Prince Fredrick as Ruler of Bãlutik?"

"I expect," the Bãlutikian Ambassador replied, "that as the Prince had no son to succeed, it will be his younger brother. He is a pleasant, rather ineffectual young man, who I regret to say has been very much taken with the French way of life rather than that of his own nation."

He spoke disparagingly, then added,

"He is married and his wife is, as she comes from Alsace, half-French. I am only hoping he will strive to adopt his brother's more disciplinarian outlook."

The Marquis thought the country would be wishing otherwise, but he was too polite to say so.

Instead, he thanked both the Ambassadors for coming to see him and promised to convey their messages to Lady Clotilda as soon as she was well enough to receive them.

As he watched them drive away down the short road, he told himself that nothing could be more fortunate, and once again a miracle had happened when he had least expected it.

He knew this meant that when he announced his marriage to Clotilda, which need not be for at least two or three months, it would seem to have come about in a normal manner.

There was no reason now why anybody should know that in order to forestall the brigands they had been married by the Abbot, and no need to explain that at the same time she had become unavailable to marry the Prince.

As he walked back up the stairs he could hardly believe that everything had turned out so well or so smoothly for both of them.

He knew that now their honeymoon would be even more perfect than it had been before.

As he neared the room where he had left Clotilda, because it was hot, he pulled off his smart, tight-fitting coat and untied the cravat around his neck.

He opened the door and Clotilda, who was standing at the window looking out to sea, turned and ran towards him.

"What has happened?" she asked. "Is it all right?"

"Everything is perfect! Completely and absolutely perfect, my precious!" the Marquis answered.

He threw his coat and the cravat down on the floor and put his arms around her.

He knew how frightened she had been that something might go wrong or that he would be taken severely to task for marrying her, since it would be difficult for anybody in England to understand the circumstances.

Then as the Marquis would have kissed her Clotilda put her fingers over his lips and said,

"Tell me first, I have been so frightened for you?"

"There was no need," the Marquis said. "The Ambassador for Bãlutik came to tell you that Prince Fredrick is dead."

"Dead?" Clotilda gasped. "I-I do not believe it!"

"It is true," the Marquis said, "and this time we have to thank the anarchists."

"What happened? I do not understand."

"You will remember the Abbot said there was at least one, if not two, anarchists among the brigands?"

"You mean it was they who killed the Prince?"

"It seems that after they learnt at the Castle what had happened, the Prince was on his way to the monastery when in that wild valley with the cliffs rising on either side of it, they threw a bomb into his carriage?"

Clotilda gave a little sigh and put her head on the Marquis's shoulder.

"Do you think I should feel sorry for him?"

"Just forget him," the Marquis said. "Personally I think he got his just deserts. All we are concerned with is the God to whom you prayed, the God who married us and has looked after us so safely that I can hardly believe I am not dreaming!"

He moved a little closer as he said,

"No one except the Abbot knows that we are married, and we are going to have a very long honeymoon together. Only when everybody has forgotten Prince Fredrick of Bãlutik, will we go back to England and announce that I am no longer an eligible bachelor."

Clotilda looked up at him.

"Oh, darling, it sounds too wonderful! And at least now there is no question of our having to annul our marriage!"

The Marquis laughed.

"That is something I never had any intention of doing and as now you are really my wife, you may be quite certain that the Vatican would not even consider it."

She turned her face up to his and he looked at her before he said,

"Do you really think I could lose you?"

"I am yours completely and absolutely yours!" Clotilda said. "Oh, darling, let us send another thanks offering to the Abbot."

"I feel at the moment like giving him everything I possess," the Marquis said, "except of course you!"

There was a touch of fire in his voice that had not been there before and, as if he thought they were wasting time standing just inside the door, he picked Clotilda up in his arms and carried her to the bed.

He laid her down gently.

Then as the sunshine coming through the window filled the whole room with glory, he was beside her.

His lips were seeking her lips, his hands were touching her body, and she could feel his heart beating frantically, urgently, demandingly against hers.

At the same time there was no hurry, for they had their whole lives ahead of them and the Marquis knew the last lingering fear that Fate might separate them had vanished.

His kisses were demanding but slow.

He kissed Clotilda's neck and her breasts until she stirred restlessly and he knew the flames of love were burning fiercely within her.

"I love you," she murmured, and her voice was more passionate than it had ever been before.

"Tell me what you feel!" the Marquis commanded.

"Wild and very, very excited."

The words came in breathless gasps.

Then with a cry that rang out into the sunshine she begged,

"Love me! Oh, my marvellous wonderful husband, love me!"

Then once again the Marquis was carrying her up into the sky and into their own special Heaven, which was theirs for all eternity.

Printed in Great Britain
by Amazon

59422185R10109